THE NORA NOTEBOOKS

THE TROUBLE WITH

ANTS

C.1

THE NORA NOTEBOOKS

THE TROUBLE WITH
ANTS

Book 1

CLAUDIA MILLS

Illustrated by Katie Kath

Alfred A. Knopf · New York

Text copyright © 2015 by Claudia Mills
Jacket art and interior illustrations copyright © 2015 by Katie Kath

All rights reserved. Published in the United States by Alfred A. Knopf, an imprint of Random House Children's Books, a division of Penguin Random House LLC, New York.

Knopf, Borzoi Books, and the colophon are registered trademarks of Penguin Random House LLC.

Visit us on the Web! randomhousekids.com

Educators and librarians, for a variety of teaching tools, visit us at RHTeachersLibrarians.com

Library of Congress Cataloging-in-Publication Data
Mills, Claudia.
The trouble with ants / Claudia Mills ; Illustrated by Katie Kath Boyd. — First edition.
pages cm. — (The Nora notebooks ; book 1)
Summary: "Science-obsessed fourth grader Nora wants to be like her scientist family and publish a professional research paper on her favorite subject: her ant farm!"—Provided by publisher
ISBN 979-0-385-39161-0 (trade) — ISBN 978-0-385-39162-7 (lib. bdg.) — ISBN 978-0-385-39164-1 (ebook)
[1. Ants—Fiction. 2. Science—Fiction. 3. Friendship—Fiction. 4. Schools—Fiction.] I. Kath, Katie, illustrator. II. Title.
PZ7.M63963Ts 2015
[Fic]—dc23
2015007380

The text of this book is set in 12.5-point New Aster.

Printed in the United States of America
September 2015
10 9 8 7 6 5 4 3 2 1

First Edition

To the incomparable Nancy Hinkel,
who caused this book to be

—C.M.

I

Nora Alpers woke up early on New Year's morning and reached for the handsome leather-bound notebook she had gotten for Christmas. The notebook had a magnetic clasp that closed with a highly satisfying *click*.

"You can use it for a diary," Nora's mother had suggested.

Nora had no intention of using the notebook as a diary. She planned on writing more interesting things in it than "Today, I had breakfast. Then I went to school. Then I went home."

"You can write stories in it," her older sister had teased. Sarah was a grown-up geologist who was expecting her first baby in a couple of months. Like everyone in Nora's family, Sarah knew Nora preferred nonfiction to fiction.

"Or poetry." Her brother, Mark, who was studying electrical engineering at MIT, had given Nora a grin.

Only her father had understood. "Nora is going to use her notebook," he had said, obviously offering a prediction, not a suggestion, "for writing down fascinating facts about ants."

Her father was absolutely, completely right.

Nora loved scribbling down all kinds of facts in all kinds of notebooks: big ones, little ones, fat ones, skinny ones, spiral ones, and now this new super-fancy one.

She had waited to start her new notebook on the first day of the new year.

"Fascinating Facts About Ants," she now wrote on the first blank page with her blue ballpoint pen. But she might write fascinating facts about other subjects, too. "And Other Extremely Interesting Things," she added.

She'd write facts she'd learned from the ant

books she checked out of the grown-up section of the library. Even better, she'd write facts she had discovered all by herself by doing experiments on the ants in her very own ant farm.

Did they accomplish more tunnel building when they were warm or cold? (Warm.) Did they build more quickly in the dark or the light? (It didn't seem to matter.) Right now she was investigating whether they dug faster in dry or wet sand. She had poured 30 milliliters (about an eighth of a cup) of water into the ant farm yesterday: not enough to drown her ants, of course, just enough to increase the moisture content of the sand. So far, they seemed to be having a harder time tunneling through the wet sand, probably because the water made it heavier. At least that was her current hypothesis.

She still had the notes she had made from her past experiments that she could copy into her notebook. And she'd learn new facts to add all the time.

This would be the Year of the Ant!

Nora thought about the Chinese calendar, which had twelve different years. It had mostly mammals in it: Year of the Rat, Ox, Tiger, Rabbit, Horse, Goat, Monkey, Dog, Pig. It had one reptile: Year of the Snake. It had one bird: Year of the Rooster. It even had one imaginary creature: Year of the Dragon. Nora didn't approve of the Year of the Dragon at all, not that you could expect scientific accuracy from astrology.

The Chinese had no year of any insect at all. No Year of the Grasshopper. No Year of the Bee. No Year of the Cockroach. If Nora had been in charge of the Chinese zodiac, she would have replaced the Year of the Dragon with the Year of the Dragonfly.

And now her own personal calendar was launching the Year of the Ant, or rather, the Year of Many, Many Ants.

Nora rummaged through her current ant library book to find an especially amazing ant fact to use as the first fact in her new notebook.

Nora's own Year of the Ant had begun.

Later that afternoon, Nora sat examining her friend Brody Baxter through the wrong end of the telescope she had gotten as another Christmas present. Brody appeared to be very tiny, very far away, and trying to get his dog to hold several tennis balls at once in his mouth.

Brody was actually a somewhat short but basically normal-sized fourth grader, seated on the floor right next to Nora in her family room. But he was indeed trying to coax his dog to fill his mouth with tennis balls.

"Just try, Dog," Brody pleaded as Dog—that was the dog's name—dropped a tennis ball onto the carpet. "The world record is five, and you're the best dog in the world, so I know you can do six."

Dog appeared to disagree. So far, he hadn't managed to hold more than one. Tennis balls scattered.

Nora set down her telescope and retrieved a tennis ball that had rolled under the couch. Her other friend who had come to visit, Mason Dixon, collected a ball that had bounced over to the table where Nora's ant farm stood. The ants didn't seem to be noticing the tennis ball commotion.

Mason and Brody were best friends and co-owners of Dog, although Dog had to live at Mason's house because of Brody's father's terrible allergies. As far as Nora could tell, both boys loved Dog equally, but Brody was vastly more enthusiastic about earning Dog a Guinness World Record. Then again, Brody was vastly more enthusiastic than Mason about everything.

"Maybe there's a different record you could try to break," Nora suggested.

From where it had been lying on the floor, she picked up the *Guinness World Records* that Brody had gotten as his favorite Christmas present and used the index to find records involving dogs. She loved books with indexes.

"'Longest tongue,'" she read aloud. "Eleven point four three centimeters. That doesn't sound *that* long."

Mason and Brody stared at her blankly. They weren't scientists the way she was; they didn't measure things using the metric system. "Four and a half inches," she translated. "Do you think Dog's tongue could be longer than four and a half inches?"

"No," said Mason.

"Yes!" said Brody. "Dog, stick out your record-breaking tongue!"

Dog was still panting enough from his tennis ball efforts that his tongue hung out partway. Nora studied what she could see of it. There was no way that Dog's tongue was four and a half inches, let alone longer. Also, where were they supposed to measure it *from*? Where did his tongue *start*? She retrieved a ruler from the drawer in the ant farm's table, because she knew Brody wouldn't believe her otherwise.

"You hold his tongue, and I'll measure," Brody told Mason.

"How about *you* hold his tongue, and *I'll* measure?" Mason countered.

"Sure." Brody was always agreeable. "I'll stretch it out as long as I can. Dog won't mind, not if he gets a world record out of it, right, Dog?"

Dog allowed Brody to hold his tongue out to its full length, but it was clear to Nora that Mason had no idea how he was supposed to go about measuring it.

"Not even close," Mason finally concluded. "Maybe three inches? It's hard to tell."

"What other records are there?" Brody asked Nora. "Pinkest tongue? Wettest tongue? Lickingest tongue?"

Nora closed the book, keeping her finger in the dog record section. In her opinion, Dog's tongue needed a rest before the boys began testing anything else about it. It was time to change the subject.

"My favorite Christmas present was my telescope. Well, my telescope and my new ant notebook. Brody's was his *Guinness World Records* book. What about you, Mason?"

"My *least* favorite was a harmonica. Tied with a book on how to juggle."

"How could your parents think you'd want to play the harmonica? Or learn to juggle?" Nora asked. "You don't like doing new things."

"*I* know that. And *they* know that. But they keep on hoping."

"Could we teach Dog to juggle?" Brody asked, with new excitement.

"No," Nora and Mason said together.

"Dog has three legs," Mason reminded Brody.

That was one of the reasons Mason and Brody

had adopted him, because nobody else had wanted to take him home from the animal shelter.

"He doesn't need four legs to juggle," Brody said. "He'll juggle with his front legs and his mouth, and he'll be the best dog juggler in the world!"

Nora sighed. She would never understand other people and their pets. Mason, who hardly liked anything, was wild about Dog. Brody, who loved everything, loved Dog most of all. Emma Averill, in their class at school, had a cat named Precious Cupcake—Nora shuddered at the name—who starred in endless cat videos Emma showed everyone on her cell phone. Emma was the only fourth grader Nora knew who had a cell phone of her own. In the most recent video, before winter break, Precious Cupcake had been wearing a Santa Claus hat while being made to dance to "Jingle Bell Rock."

Nora's gaze fell fondly on her ant farm. Ants were such sensible pets. They didn't wear comical hats or do holiday dances. They stayed content in their tidy glass enclosure: independent, self-reliant, busy, and endlessly interesting.

"All right," Nora said, turning back to the *Guinness* book. "Here's another dog record: how many steps can a dog walk while balancing a cup of water on his head without spilling it?"

Brody leaped to his feet. "Do you have a glass? Will your parents mind if we spill a little water?"

"Dog has three legs," Mason reminded Brody again. "Walking with a cup of water on your head is harder if you don't have as many legs as other people—I mean, other dogs."

Brody's already bright face brightened even more. "*That* can be the record! Most steps taken with a glass of water balanced on the head of a dog with three legs!"

Nora shook her head. "That's too *specific* a record. Too narrow a category. There aren't enough three-legged dogs carrying glasses of water on their heads for it to be worth setting a record about."

"So what else is there?" Brody persisted.

Nora shrugged. She had already flipped to the section on ants. There was a record for largest ant farm, but what kind of a dumb record was that? What did the *size* of an ant farm matter? It was what ants *did* in their farm that counted. And even if her ants proved to be faster at tunnel building than other people's ants, that wouldn't be what

Nora cared about. She'd want to know *why* they were so fast. It was the science behind the record that was worth thinking about. *Why* did one dog have such a long tongue? *How* did another dog carry so many tennis balls in its mouth or balance a glass of water so carefully on its head?

"Maybe we need to come up with our own record," Brody suggested. "Not a record that's already in the book for Dog to break, but a new record that nobody ever thought up before."

"Like what?" Mason sounded skeptical.

"Like—like—Nora, you're really good at thinking things up."

It was true. But, frankly, Nora greatly doubted that there was anything at all that Dog was best in the world at doing. After all, it couldn't be easy to be best in the world at something, or else everyone would be that good, and then it wouldn't be *best* anymore.

"Can Dog learn how to play the harmonica?" Brody asked.

"No," Nora and Mason said together.

Nora kept on thumbing through the pages of Brody's book. It was amazing how many records people held for all kinds of strange things: largest collection of rubber ducks, most spoons balanced on the face, farthest distance to spit milk.

She hoped Brody wouldn't decide to train Dog in milk spitting, at least not this afternoon, at her house.

Then her eyes fell upon another world record: youngest person ever to have a research paper published in a peer-reviewed science journal. The person was a girl named Emily Rosa. Emily Rosa had been eleven when she published her record-breaking paper.

Nora was ten.

She hardly listened as Brody asked Mason if Dog could get a record for *chewing* tennis balls, given that Dog had already destroyed two tennis balls in the last half hour.

Had Emily Rosa loved science since she had been old enough to love anything?

Did Emily Rosa have the periodic table of the elements and a map of all the constellations, both Northern and Southern Hemispheres, hanging on the wall of her bedroom?

Did Emily Rosa know how to fix a broken vacuum cleaner?

Did Emily Rosa have her own telescope?

Nora had already done months of experiments with her ant farm and documented them all in a special science notebook. She was probably already the leading ten-year-old expert on myrmecology, the scientific study of ants. She had been looking for a worthy goal for the new year, and now she had found it: to be the youngest person ever to publish an article in a grown-up science journal.

She glanced over again at her busy, bustling ants, burrowing through their nicely moistened sand. They had no idea how important they were soon going to be to the future of science.

A worker ant is less than one-millionth the size of a human being. But all of the ants in the world taken together weigh as much as all the human beings in the world. See what I mean about how amazing ants are?

School started again the next day. Nora didn't mind that winter break was over. She liked her fourth-grade teacher, an enthusiastic, sports-loving man who called himself Coach Joe. Coach Joe had told Nora once that he'd like her to bring her ant farm to school to show their class. Maybe she should plan to do that soon.

As she stood outside Plainfield Elementary School in the early-morning cold waiting for the bell, she heard a shriek.

"Dunk! Stop that! Dunk! No!"

Nora recognized that shriek. It could belong to only one shrieker: Emma Averill.

Dunk, the biggest, beefiest boy in their class, had scooped up a handful of snow from the shoveled mounds by the side of the blacktop.

"Here's some nice clean snow, Emma!" he called out, holding up his snowball for all to see. "Your face looks a little dirty. Don't you think it could use a good washing?"

Emma shrieked again. It wasn't a bloodcurdling shriek, more of a cross between a shriek and a giggle.

Mason and Brody had arrived, inseparable as usual, joining the crowd of Coach Joe's fourth graders surrounding Dunk and Emma.

"Why is Dunk picking on Emma?" Brody asked indignantly.

"Because he's mean," Mason replied.

Nora stared at both of them. Hadn't they seen any shows on the Animal Planet channel? Boy penguins made strange cries and flapped their flippers to attract girl penguins. Boy lions ruffled their manes to attract girl lions. And boy humans threatened to wash the faces of girl humans with handfuls of snow.

"Dunk is acting that way because he *likes* Emma," Nora explained. "And Emma is shrieking so loudly because she likes Dunk."

Brody looked doubtful. Mason looked shocked. Nora knew Mason was thinking: *how could* anybody *like* Dunk?

The bell rang. Nora made her way into Coach Joe's room, Emma's shrieks still ringing in her ears.

Coach Joe's class always began with a "huddle" on the football-shaped rug in the back corner of the room.

"Welcome back, team!" Coach Joe said. "Everyone ready for some championship play? Grand slams? Slam dunks?" He grinned at Dunk, who had wedged himself next to Emma. "Touchdowns?"

Coach Joe clearly liked sports metaphors. Nora herself played on a YMCA basketball team with Mason, Brody, and her friends Elise, Tamara, and Amy. Elise loved writing the way Nora loved science. Tamara loved jazz dance and hip-hop. Amy, who wanted to be a vet someday, loved animals, though Nora hadn't been able to convince Amy to share her own fondness for ants. All of them loved basketball, even if their team, the Fighting Bulldogs, really should have been named the Losing Bulldogs.

The other kids clapped in response to Coach Joe's greeting, except for Mason, who didn't go in for clapping. Nora wasn't a big clapper, either, but she gave a nod of approval. It would definitely be a grand slam, slam dunk, and touchdown when she published an article about her ants in a grown-up science journal.

"Social studies!" Coach Joe went on. "So far this school year, we've learned about Native Americans, the age of exploration, and the settling of the thirteen colonies. So you know what's coming, don't you?"

Most of Nora's classmates looked blank.

Someone had to say something, so she raised her hand.

"The American Revolution."

"Exactly!" Coach Joe beamed at Nora, as if she had said something brilliant instead of the most obvious thing in the world. "The Sons of Liberty.

The Boston Tea Party. Battles. More battles. The Declaration of Independence. Washington crossing the Delaware. The terrible winter at Valley Forge. Yes, pretty soon we're going to see our colonists with a brand-new country."

Leaning toward Emma, Dunk gave a loud burp that he clearly thought any fourth-grade girl would find irresistible.

"Dunk," Coach Joe said, without even casting a look in his direction.

The burping ceased.

"In language arts," Coach Joe continued, "we'll be taking a page from the colonists' playbook and writing our own persuasive speeches. The revolution wasn't won primarily with muskets and cannons, you know. It was won with words. 'These are the times that try men's souls.' 'Give me liberty or give me death.' 'We hold these truths to be self-evident, that all men are created equal.'"

Nora didn't think of herself as a word person— she planned to write her ant farm article in plain, simple words that told about her ant experiments in a plain, simple way—but the stirring lines Coach Joe had quoted did give her a strange, shimmery feeling inside. She could see how they could make someone feel like launching a revolution.

"So we'll be working on learning how to write our own persuasive speeches," Coach Joe concluded.

"What are we going to be trying to persuade people to do?" Mason asked. Nora knew Mason was tired of listening to speeches from his parents, which were intended to persuade him to try new things.

"Anything you like," Coach Joe replied. "You can pretend to be a colonist and help the cause of rebellion. You can pretend to be a Tory and defend the rule of King George the Third. You can write a persuasive letter to your congressional representative. After all, we wouldn't even have congressional representatives if it weren't for the persuasive speeches of the American Revolution. How about a speech to convince your parents to let you stay up late to watch your favorite TV show? Or a speech to convince me to give you less homework—good luck on that one! Write about whatever matters most to *you*."

Nora didn't know yet what she'd write about.

She did know that her persuasive speech would rely on facts—hard, cold, true facts—rather than on fancy phrases. She wouldn't write lines like "Give me liberty or give me death." She'd list the pros and cons of liberty, and the pros and cons of death, and count up the pros and cons on each side, and see which side added up to the biggest number. Nothing was more persuasive than math.

"All right, team," Coach Joe said. "Huddle's over. Time for the back-to-school after-winter-break kickoff."

At lunch, Nora sat with the other girls on her basketball team, as well as with Emma and Emma's best friend, Bethy. She would have sat with Mason and Brody sometimes, but in the cafeteria at Plainfield Elementary School, fourth-grade girls and fourth-grade boys never sat together. There was no rule that said it had to be that way, but everyone seemed to know that was how it had to be.

Nora understood. In the animal kingdom, the females of many species lived separately from the males for much of the time: seals, elk, mink. On the other hand, no female member of the animal kingdom ever expected another female member of the animal kingdom to squeal over her latest cat videos.

As Nora carried her tray over to their table, Bethy was hunched together with Tamara, Elise, and Amy, all peering at the tiny screen on Emma's phone. Plainfield Elementary had a rule against calling or texting during school hours, but apparently there was no policy against using your phone at lunchtime to make other people watch videos of your cat.

"Oh!" Bethy gushed.

"That's not even the cutest one," Emma announced, taking control of her phone. "The cutest one—wait till you see it—the cutest one is the one I'm calling 'Princess Precious.' Okay, here it is."

Beaming, Emma handed the phone back to Bethy so that the other girls could resume their peering.

"I love her cape!" Elise gave a sigh of admiration.

"Pink is definitely her color," Tamara agreed.

Amy exchanged a glance with Nora; Nora knew

Amy didn't approve of costumes for pets. But Amy asked politely, "Where did you find a cat tiara?"

All the girls seemed to act differently around Emma. Nora would hardly recognize them as the same girls who could knock a basketball out of someone else's hands and barrel down the court for a layup.

But right here, right now, there was no escaping Precious Cupcake. Nora leaned in closer to behold Emma's cat dressed in a jeweled beauty-queen crown and a cape of pink velvet trimmed with purple ribbon.

"What breed of cat is she?" Nora asked. Probably American shorthair. Amy looked eager to hear the answer to Nora's question, too.

Emma shrugged, obviously less interested in the biological classification of her cat than in her costumed cuteness.

"They should put her picture in the dictionary next to the word *cute*!" Bethy exclaimed.

"Here's another one," Emma said. "I'm calling this one 'Cupcake Capers.' I take back what I said before: *this* one is the cutest."

Out of the corner of her eye, Nora caught a

glimpse of Precious Cupcake licking the frosting off an actual cupcake. Not a healthy food choice for cats, that was for sure. But even future vet Amy made no comment.

"Nora, you can see it first this time," Emma told her.

"That's okay," Nora said. "I don't mind waiting."

Maybe the end-of-lunch bell would ring before it was her turn to admire the Cupcake Capers of Precious Cupcake. Luckily, right now the squealers were too busy squealing to notice that she wasn't squealing, too. So Nora gratefully tuned out the

gushing and sighing of her friends, and sat thinking of more fascinating facts about ants that she
could write in her special notebook.

The total population of ants in the world
is ten thousand trillion. To write a number
that big, you'd have to write a one
followed by 16 zeroes! Which looks like this:
10,000,000,000,000,000.

It was hard now for Nora to remember a time when she didn't have an ant farm. But actually it had been only a few months ago that ants first came into her life in a serious way.

She had always liked watching ants in nature. She'd be out on a walk on a summer afternoon, and there on the sidewalk would be a swarm of ants, thousands of them, crowded so thickly together that half a square of concrete was black with them. Why were they there now, when they hadn't been there a day ago? Had an ant scout located some unexpected treat or danger, and alerted the others? How did they communicate? What kinds of things did they communicate about?

Toward the end of third grade, her parents had helped her order an ant farm on the Internet, along with a tube of ants.

Nora had studied the website that described what they'd be getting.

"'Live arrival guaranteed,'" she read to her mother as she sat at the computer in her mother's office at the university. Both her parents were scientists. Her dad was a biochemist, and her mother was an astrophysicist. They joked that he liked to study tiny things very close up and she liked to study enormous things very far away.

Nora kept on reading from the ant farm website.

"But they say they can guarantee live arrival only if the temperature isn't below forty degrees or above eighty-five. How hot is it going to be"—she checked the estimated delivery date if she placed her order today—"three days from now?"

Her mother pulled up the weather on her phone. "High of eighty-six. What do you think? Take a chance on them anyway?"

Nora knew that the hopeful look in her mother's

eyes meant that she wanted Nora's answer to be no. Her mother, who was one of the country's foremost scientific experts on the rings of Saturn, had a most unscientific aversion to bugs, including ladybugs, which even Emma didn't mind.

Nora nodded. "I want to go ahead and order them. Now that it's almost summer, it's only going to be getting hotter and hotter."

Her ants were just going to have to deal with the weather, whatever it was. After all, ants lived outside in the world in all temperatures, freezing cold to blazing hot. Of course, in the outside world they lived underground in their snug little tunnels. Still, Nora was sure she had seen ants swarming on the pavement on days when the temperature soared past eighty-five degrees.

She did feel nervous three days later, when she came home from school and retrieved the small carton from the mailbox.

Would her ants be alive or dead?

"Be alive!" she beamed the command toward the package, even though she knew she couldn't make any difference in their aliveness just by willing it with all her might.

In the kitchen, she cut through the tape on the

box with a pair of shears and opened the lid. From a heap of Styrofoam peanuts, she pulled out the plastic ant farm, a bit disappointed by how silly it looked, with its green plastic houses, barn, silo, and windmill. As if ants would care about any of that! An ant farm wasn't really a *farm*. No one had ever sung *"E-I-E-I-O"* about ants. At least Nora was pretty sure that was the case.

Where *were* the ants?

Digging deeper into the Styrofoam peanuts, she grasped a small tube.

Filled with ants.

Filled with ants that were . . . alive! Ants that were not only alive but apparently eager to get out. Ants that, in fact, looked quite angry—not that Nora believed you could attribute human emotions to ants. But if you could, if ants did have the same feelings that people did, these ants resembled people who were very, very irritated at having spent the last few days in uncomfortably warm temperatures, cooped up in a little plastic tube.

The instructions said to put the ants in the re-frigerator for ten minutes to calm them down before transferring them into their new home. They'd probably enjoy that anyway.

The instructions said that the ants in the tube were western harvester ants.

The instructions also said that western harvester ants were stinging ants.

"Dad," Nora said as her father wandered into the kitchen to refill his coffee cup. "They sent us stinging ants. The instructions say that my ants 'can inflict a painful sting.'"

Her dad looked sober, even though he was a fellow insect lover. "Your mother isn't wild about ants to start with," he said in a low voice. "I don't think she's going to be pleased with the idea of stinging ants."

"What am I not going to be pleased with?" came Nora's mother's voice from the kitchen doorway.

"Oh, nothing. Look, Mom, they're here!" Nora made her own voice cheerful, so her mother would get into the proper ant-loving mood. "My ants are here, and they *are* alive!"

"Oh goody," her mother replied.

Neither Nora nor her father made any mention about painful stings.

"So where are they?" her mother asked uneasily.

Nora held up the tube. Her mother shrank back, as if the ants might leap out and start marching all over the kitchen, bent on conquest.

"We need to put them in the fridge first," Nora explained, "to calm them down."

"Well, I do greatly prefer calm ants to agitated ones," her mother said. "But ants in the refrigerator? I can't believe it's healthy to put a tube of ants right next to our family's food supply."

"They won't get out," Nora reassured her.

"Says who?"

"Says me. They can't get out. Look, the stopper is in nice and tight."

To demonstrate, Nora turned the ant tube upside down to show how snugly the stopper was in place.

"Oh, Nora, I really don't think—"

"It's fine! Mom, the ant company isn't going to ship ants in a tube with a loose stopper." *Especially painfully stinging ants.*

For a further demonstration, Nora wiggled the stopper a bit and then gave the upside-down tube of ants a good shake.

"See?"

But what she saw next, what they all saw, was the stopper popping out.

Large red ants—large, red, seemingly angry stinging ants—scattered all over the kitchen floor.

Nora's mother screamed.

"Catch them! Nora! Neil! Catch them!"

It would definitely be a good idea to catch them. On that, Nora and her mother were in complete agreement. The question was: how?

For the next twenty minutes, Nora and her father tried to collect the ants, one by one, scooping them into empty jars from the recycling bin. But the ants didn't want to be scooped. And sometimes one that had already been scooped became unscooped and made its way out as another ant was being coaxed to make its way in.

Nora's mother had fled to the safety of the dining room. She kept calling unhelpful things like "Be sure you get them all!" and "It's all right just to kill them if you need to!"

Nora was trying to tune out this unwelcome advice when one of the painfully stinging ants gave a painful sting to the tip of her index finger.

"Ow!" she couldn't help but yell. "Ow!"

"What is it? What happened?" her mother called.

"It's okay," her father called back.

"It doesn't sound okay."

Her mother reappeared in the kitchen doorway as Nora was sucking her stung finger.

Concern for Nora gave her mom new courage. Heedless of any remaining escaped ants, she rushed over to examine Nora's finger.

"Oh, this looks bad. What kind of ants *are* these?"

When no one answered, she snatched up the instructions from the counter. "*Stinging ants?* They sent you *stinging* ants?"

That had definitely been a terrible afternoon.

Nora's father took over as the sole ant re-capturer, leaving Nora's mother to administer first aid for the sting. In the end, twenty ants were deposited into the ant farm, to settle into the soft white sand that Nora had already put in place to welcome them, moistened with a quarter cup of water. The few remaining ants were never seen again, except for one that provoked a scream from her mother a day or two later and got itself squished to death with a wadded paper towel.

Holding no hard feelings toward her ants—you couldn't blame a stinging ant for stinging any more than you could blame a singing bird for singing— Nora did her best to care for them, giving them little bits of apple or cracker to eat and making sure they had a few drops of water to drink every couple of days.

For the first week, the ants did all the things that Nora had hoped they would do: they built tunnels, carried morsels of food off to eat and digest, stayed busy in useful ant ways.

But then they started dying. And kept on dying. And soon they were all dead.

Maybe Nora had fed them too much or too little? Or maybe they were just at the end of their life expectancy. Without a queen, they couldn't reproduce and create new baby ants to keep the colony going. The instructions had said that it was against the law for the ant farm company to send a queen through the mail. Nora had no idea who would make a law like that, or why.

Her ants were dead and done for. But Nora wasn't done with ants.

On the Internet, she learned that she could make

her own ant farm, using a rectangular, flat terrarium from a pet or craft store. She could use dirt from her own backyard. And she could find her own ants to live in it.

She had no trouble finding ants. Nora was good at noticing things like where dirt was mounded in a corner of the yard to form an anthill. It was harder finding a queen: the large, winged ant that hatched all the eggs that became all the ants that would keep the colony going. Queens didn't sit out in plain view on ant-sized thrones, with ant-sized crowns on their heads. They were hidden deep inside the colony, protected by soldier ants. No matter how long she watched and waited, Nora never saw any queen ready for capture.

Maybe it would have been wrong to capture a queen anyway. Maybe that's why ant farm companies weren't allowed to ship queens through the mail. The other ants would be asking, "Where's our queen? Where did she go? Oh, Your Majesty, what has become of you?"

No. Ants didn't ask questions like that. They didn't really think at all. Their brains were too small for thinking. In any case, Nora never found a queen.

But her second colony of ants lived longer than the first, mail-order colony of ants. And when they died off, she just went out and found more.

And now she was ready for her year of serious scientific ant experiments to begin.

Ant queens live a long time. The queens of most species live 5 years or longer. The record for a queen's life span is 30 years! But lots of queens die before they ever get to found a colony. For every queen that succeeds in starting a colony, hundreds or thousands die trying. I would love to have an ant queen someday more than anything in the world.

As soon as she got to her house that afternoon, Nora checked on her ants. Some days, she took the bus from school to a parent's office at the university and did homework there until they were ready to leave. On other days, one parent was working at home, grading exams or doing something on the computer, so she could walk home directly from school. This was a walk-home day.

Whenever she checked her ant farm after a whole day away at school, she always found that something had changed. New tunnels had appeared.

Food had been eaten. A deceased ant had been carried off to the corner of the farm where her ants stored their dead.

Today, she arrived home halfway through an ant funeral. Two ants were lugging the corpse of a third down a long tunnel to reach the ant graveyard.

Rest in peace, little ant.

Nora considered recording the ant burial with her parents' old video camera. *That* would be something to show the other girls at lunch tomorrow. *That* would be a pleasant change from the Precious Cupcake costume parade. But she wasn't going to let herself start imitating Emma, even if Amy might enjoy a change in video subjects, too.

It might be a good idea, however, to start documenting her ants' activities. She could record them for the sake of science, not for lunchtime show-and-tell. If she studied the videos, she might get an idea for her groundbreaking experiment. She couldn't publish a scientific article on the usual science-fair stuff that any kid with an ant farm had already found on ant farm websites. She had to come up with something that science had never seen before.

Nora filmed her ants for a while. Then she did homework: some easy math problems, and reading a chapter in her huge social studies textbook on the American Revolution. She already knew that she wasn't going to be reading about any women who did important things to help the cause of freedom. Most of the famous women back then were famous because they were married to famous men. That wasn't how Nora planned on becoming famous as a scientist.

Neither of her parents were really famous scientists, but her mother was more famous than her father, even if her father kept a calmer, more scientific head when stinging western harvester ants were on the loose in the kitchen. Her mother was on TV occasionally, when the rings of Saturn made the national news. Admittedly, that wasn't often. If Nora were in charge of the news, she'd lead off every night with stories like "New Discovery About the Chemical Composition of Stars!" and "Breakthrough in Ant Farm Research!"

Maybe that's what she should write her persuasive speech about: why the news should have more science stories.

Emma would probably write hers about how the news should have more cat videos.

Nora smiled at the thought.

But then her smile disappeared. Even if her speech was a better speech, her classmates would probably end up being more persuaded by Emma's. Persuasive speeches could only go so far and do so much. First, people had to be willing to be persuaded.

It was definitely time for her to bring her farm to school to show Coach Joe's class the wonder of ants.

The next day and the day after that, it was unseasonably warm for January, with highs in the sixties.

Global climate change, Nora thought to herself darkly.

But warmer temperatures were good for transporting an ant farm to school. She had confirmed with Coach Joe that she could present her ant farm during science on Friday. Ants had nothing to do with electromagnetism, their current subject of study, but Coach Joe said ants would make a nice change.

"Kids will still get a *charge* out of them," he told Nora.

She was so surprised to hear him making a science pun rather than a sports reference that she forgot to give a polite chuckle.

Nora's father drove her to school on Friday so she wouldn't jostle her ant farm or risk tripping and shattering months of her ants' hard work. She kept the farm covered with an old T-shirt. While she didn't think of herself as a dramatic person, she wanted to introduce her ants to the class with some fanfare. She suspected that a lot of people, unbelievable as it might seem, thought ants were boring.

Ants? Boring?!

So she wanted the equivalent of a drumroll before she uncovered the farm to their astonished eyes.

She didn't wait on the blacktop for the bell. Instead, she hurried to Coach Joe's room and set the ant farm safely on the bookcase in the back of the room, where it wouldn't be disturbed.

Coach Joe was at his desk when she arrived.

"The ants go marching two by two, hurrah, hurrah!" he sang out in greeting.

Nora had forgotten about that kindergarten song. She was glad there was a song about ants, but of course the ants in the song did the most un-ant-like things imaginable. "The little one stops to suck his thumb." As if ants had thumbs rather than mandibles! "The little one stops to tie his shoe." Tying a shoe? Really?

Still, Nora gave Coach Joe a smile. He meant well.

"Nora, I'm thinking it might work better to let you show your ants during the morning huddle. What do you think?"

"Sure," Nora agreed. Now that her ants were here at school, the sooner she could show them to everybody, the better.

Maybe Emma would want to start taking ant videos? Or at least watching them once in a while? Wouldn't that be a lovely change at lunchtime?

The bell rang. Nora's audience came racing into Coach Joe's room, Dunk leading the way with his shouts and swagger.

One tiny worry wormed itself into Nora's brain.

Dunk had a tendency to be a bully. He'd better not even think about bullying her ants!

Once morning announcements had been read, the Pledge of Allegiance recited, and "You're a Grand Old Flag" sung, Coach Joe called the class into their Friday huddle. Nora carried the T-shirt-covered object from the bookcase to the football-shaped rug. She sat down and settled it safely on her lap, stroking its T-shirt cover as if to reassure her ants before their big moment.

"What's that?" Mason asked warily.

"You'll see," Nora replied.

"Is it a treat to share? Is it something to eat?" Brody asked hopefully.

"No!"

She knew that people did eat ants in many parts of the world: Asia, South America, sub-Saharan Africa. There was no reason why the protein found in insects shouldn't be a food source for human beings as well as for other species. But she didn't want anybody eating *her* ants.

"Good morning, team," Coach Joe said in his usual hearty way. "Dunk, I'm not sure you're making the best choice about where to sit."

All week long, Dunk had plopped himself down next to Emma during the morning huddle and poked her with the eraser end of his pencil, yanked off her flowered headband, and threatened to remove his shoes so she'd have to smell his feet.

"So, Dunk, why don't you come over here and sit next to me?"

Scowling, Dunk obeyed.

"This morning, Nora has brought something fascinating to show to us. Something that has to do with science, because it's part of the natural world, but also has to do with social studies, because it can teach us a lot about how a colony needs to function. It even has to do with art, you might say, as what she's showing us is a pretty amazing work of art, too."

Coach Joe couldn't have given a better introduction if Nora had written it herself. It was a powerfully persuasive speech about the marvels of ants. And he had done a wonderful job of not revealing exactly what was still hidden under the T-shirt. He had left her the fun of revealing the final surprise.

"Nora," Coach Joe said, as her cue.

Nora smiled at her classmates. Mason and Brody would already know the surprise by now. They had both seen her ants at her house many times. So she focused her smiling on the other girls, especially Emma.

"What I have to show you," Nora said slowly, to prolong the suspense for one more sweet moment, "is . . ."

One last smile for good measure.

"My ant farm!"

She whisked off the T-shirt to reveal her scurrying ants in all their glory.

Emma shrieked. Not a giggling shriek this time, but a shriek of pure terror, horror, and loathing.

A few of the other girls joined in the screaming. Shrieking, it turned out, was contagious, a phenomenon some scientist should study sometime.

But Nora was not that scientist.

And now was not that time.

Emma fled from the huddle to the safety of her desk, as if the ants were loose instead of confined to an ant farm, and were painfully stinging ants instead of gentle ants from Nora's own backyard. Dunk dashed after Emma, pretending that he was

about to put an ant down the back of her pink-flowered top. Bethy followed as well, to try to get between Dunk and Emma, with Tamara and Elise trailing behind. Most of the other kids gathered around them, howling with laughter.

"Team!" Coach Joe bellowed. "Team, calm down!"

It did no good.

The only kids left in the huddle were three or four kids who also loved science, plus Amy, Mason, and Brody, Nora's most loyal friends.

Nora blinked back tears. She wasn't going to cry just because other people were totally ridiculous! But she felt—she tried to analyze what her emotions were right now—she felt *hurt*. Hurt on behalf of her ants. Hurt on behalf of science itself.

Coach Joe left his stool and stood facing the rest of the class.

"Team," he said somberly. "I have to say, you dropped the ball on this one. Nora, I'm sorry."

"That's okay," Nora said, covering up her ant farm with the T-shirt again.

Her classmates had made it clear: they hadn't yet been persuaded to like ants. But she'd be willing to bet that the editors of some famous, fancy science journal were soon going to let the world know that they liked her ants a *lot*.

Ants communicate in lots of different ways. One way is by using pheromones, which are chemical secretions they can taste and smell. Does Dunk think his smelly feet have pheromones to make Emma like him?

Nora refused to sit at her usual table that day at lunch. She took her sack lunch from home and headed outside to eat beneath the winter-bare trees. Kids were allowed to go outside for lunch recess whenever they were done in the cafeteria. Today, Nora was done from minute one.

Even though it was early January, the sun was so warm that she wasn't a bit chilly as she perched on the picnic table in her jacket and knit hat.

She was touched when Amy abandoned the other girls and came out to join her.

"If only Emma hadn't screamed," Amy said sorrowfully.

"I know."

"Sometimes I wish Emma weren't so . . . Emma-ish," Amy said.

"Me, too."

But Nora knew Emma was going to keep on being Emma-ish, just as she was going to keep on being Nora-ish. She wasn't really mad at Emma for screaming any more than she had been mad at her stinging ants for stinging. Both people and ants were what they were and did what they did. But if only people could be and do something different!

"Game tomorrow," Amy said, her voice more cheery. "We're playing the Killer Whales."

Dunk's team.

"Maybe we should change the name of our team," Amy suggested. "From the Fighting Bull-dogs to the Stinging Ants."

Nora laughed. She had told Amy the story about her first try at setting up an ant farm. "We'd be sure to win, then," she joked.

Besides, they had beaten Dunk's team once last fall. They could do it again tomorrow.

During the game the next morning, Nora didn't let herself think about ant experiments or cat videos. She focused her thoughts on positioning herself to shoot and on guarding one of Dunk's teammates, who was almost as big and beefy as Dunk himself.

At one point, as she was preparing to take a free throw after one Killer Whale had fouled her, she heard Dunk's taunt: "Ant lover!"

Apparently, Dunk thought that was an insult!

Nora showed him what a perfect shot an ant lover could make.

The Fighting Bulldogs, aka the Stinging Ants, won, 16–14.

At home that afternoon, Nora tried to think of the next experiment to do with her ants, the experiment that would make her name as a rising young scientist.

Was it cheating to ask her scientist parents for some ideas? Should a soon-to-be-famous scientist come up with breakthrough ideas all on her own, or was it all right to ask for help from other scientists?

Nora remembered a famous line said by one of the most famous scientists of all time: Sir Isaac Newton. One day, an apple fell on his head, and as he asked himself why it had fallen down rather than up, he discovered the law of gravity. So he had certainly had help from the apple. The famous line he had said was "If I have seen further (than others), it is by standing on the shoulders of giants." He didn't mean that he actually stood on the shoulders of tall people. He meant that his ideas had built on the ideas of the great scientists who had come before him.

Nora found her father at his extremely messy desk in his extremely messy upstairs office. That was another difference between her parents. Her father's desk was buried under stacks of paper piled every which way. Even the floor was barely visible, covered with a jumble of books, science journals, heaps of student final exams from last semester. Nora could hardly walk across the room without causing some pile of paper to topple. In contrast, her mother's office was as neat as could be, her desk

completely bare except for her laptop, a vase of flowers, and one coffee cup. Right now Nora could see
that her father's desk had six or seven coffee cups
on it—each one, she knew, half filled with coffee he
had poured but forgotten to drink.

Nora was neat like her mother, not messy like
her father. She liked her mother's office vastly better than she liked her father's office. But her father was the better parent to go to with a question
about ants.

"Is it cheating if I ask you to help me come up

with an idea for the best ant farm experiment ever?" she asked.

There was no place to sit down in her dad's office—his couch was occupied with the same mess that spread over every other available surface. So she stood next to his desk while she waited for his answer to her question.

Her father thought for a while before replying. No matter what question she asked, he never answered right away.

"You'll still be the one doing the experiment," he finally said. "And interpreting the results. If you were to publish your findings"—*how did he know?!*—"it would be intellectually honest to have a footnote thanking anyone who helped you in your work. So you could say, 'I am grateful to Professor Neil Alpers for the suggestion to pursue this line of research.'"

Nora liked that wording. She could so easily imagine it in print.

"Can I have a piece of paper to write that down?" she asked.

"Sure. If there's one thing I have, it's pieces of paper. Finding a blank one, on the other hand, might not be so easy."

After some rummaging, he handed her a scrap of paper, somewhat stained from coffee, and a pencil. Nora scribbled down the words he had told her.

"So what *would* be a good line of research to pursue?" she asked.

He paused again to think. "You could take a few of the ants out of the farm," he said. "Put them in a measured area and see how long it takes them to find a piece of food placed outside the area. You'd be studying the ants in relation to both time and distance. You could keep increasing the distance of the food from their starting point. Is there some distance that is too far? Or will they keep seeking until they find what they are looking for?"

It was a perfect idea! Except for . . .

"Mom," Nora said. "She's not going to go in for taking the ants out of the ant farm. You know she's not."

"Good point." Another pause. "You can do it on one of her university days. Just make sure you put the experiment ants inside a larger enclosure so they don't get out. Like—the bathtub, maybe."

Nora didn't think her mother would like ants in the bathtub, either. But she'd use the bathtub in her own bathroom, not her parents' bathroom. Besides, science called for some sacrifices.

Just as Nora was measuring the dimensions of the bathtub, the phone rang. She was the only one in her family who ever answered the phone, as both of her parents got all their important calls on their cell phones and Nora didn't have a cell phone yet.

"Hello?"

"Nora, can you come over? Right away?"

It was Mason, sounding more upset than she had ever heard him before.

"What happened? Is it Dog? Is Dog okay?"

"Dog's been skunked!"

Ants can leave lots of different messages with their pheromones. They can warn other ants about danger. They can tell other ants where to find food. Thing to find out: does skunk spray contain pheromones?

Although the afternoon had been as unseasonably warm as the rest of the week, darkness was falling and the night air was frosty as Nora hurried to Mason's house, a few blocks away. She could smell the pungent odor of skunk, stronger than her father's strongest coffee, as soon as she turned the corner onto Mason's street. How could one small animal produce such an enormous stink? What was that smelly stuff *made* of? What chemicals combined to make a stink so horrific?

By the time she reached Mason's house, which

was right next door to Brody's house, Nora's eyes were stinging and her nose was crinkling. She could see the boys outside, crouched next to Dog in the pool of bright light from the light fixture over the garage door.

It was one of the saddest sights she had ever seen.

Mason was trying to get Dog not to rub the spray from his face with his paws, as Brody sat next to him with streaming eyes—whether from the skunk smell or from tears, Nora couldn't tell.

"Don't, Dog," Mason pleaded. "You'll just make it worse."

"Where are your parents?" Nora asked.

"They're out on a date night with Brody's parents," Mason said. "Cammie and Cara are 'babysitting.'"

Cammie and Cara were Brody's older sisters, who were nowhere in sight.

"They're inside," Brody explained, "trying to call my parents or Mason's parents to find out what to do."

"What we need to do," Nora said, "is wash Dog. Now."

"In the bathtub?" Mason asked.

Nora could tell he was wondering if his mother would really want Dog inside the house, dragged all the way up the carpeted staircase to the upstairs bathroom. A skunked dog would be a worse thing to find in your bathtub than a few little ants.

"No. We don't need to wash all of him. In fact, we don't *want* to wash all of him. We don't want to get the stinky stuff on his front half all over the fur that doesn't stink yet, or then all of him will stink."

"What do we wash him with?" Brody asked.

"Hydrogen peroxide."

"Whatever that is," Mason said. "Which we probably don't have. And can't get, because none of us can drive anywhere to get it."

Cammie and Cara came back outside. They were both in middle school and even more giggly than Emma herself. But neither one was giggling now.

"They're not answering their phones!" Cammie wailed. "They went to some dumb classical music concert and turned their phones off!"

"They don't even care that we're here all by ourselves trying to figure out what to do with the world's stinkiest dog!" Cara moaned.

"Do you have any hydrogen peroxide?" Nora interrupted.

Brody's sisters stopped their wailing and moaning, and gave Nora a look of utter confusion.

"Yes," Cammie said. "I use it to put highlights in my hair. You want some *now*? Anyway, that kind of highlight will look strange in dark hair like yours. It'll make you look—"

"Like a skunk," Cara finished the sentence.

Nora rolled her eyes. "Hydrogen peroxide," she explained, "helps neutralize the smell from a skunk."

"Oh!" Cammie started to race inside Brody's house to get it.

"There's other stuff we need, too," Nora called after her. Cammie waited to hear the rest. "Baking soda? I think we need baking soda. And a bucket of water. And a sponge, of course, to wash him. But first we need to look up how much hydrogen peroxide we need and how much baking soda, and if there's any other ingredients to add."

Cara was already searching for it on her phone. "A bottle of hydrogen peroxide. I think we have almost a full bottle. And a quarter cup of baking soda. I know my mom has some baking soda somewhere. And we need some dish detergent. And some warm water, too."

The sisters headed back inside together, on a mission now.

"It's my fault," Brody said, in a small voice, as Dog lay whimpering beside him. "I'm the one who wanted to take him for one more walk, because it was such a nice day. He pulled away before I could get the leash on and ran after something. I thought it was a squirrel or a rabbit, and I yelled at him to stop. But . . ."

He didn't need to finish the sentence.

Nora pulled off her hat and held it over her nose to block out some of the smell. Her eyes still stung.

"Poor Dog," she said. "How could Dog get skunked in *January*? I thought skunks weren't very active in the winter. I read that in a library book over winter break."

"I guess this skunk can't read," Mason muttered.

Maybe the warmer weather this past week had made the skunk think it was spring. But spring in January appeared to be over. A gust of bitter wind made Nora shiver.

Cammie and Cara reappeared with the ingredients for Dog's de-skunking bath and the bucket to mix them in.

Nora took charge of the mixing. It was like an experiment with her chemistry set. The peroxide made the liquid in the bucket fizzle.

"Okay," she said. "It's ready."

"Here, Dog," Mason said gently. "Brody and I are going to make that awful smell go away."

He dipped a sponge into the peroxide mixture and started wiping Dog's face and shoulders. Brody took a second sponge and wiped Dog from the other side.

Dog whimpered again. He looked better now, without any of that oozy gunk on him. Nora couldn't tell if he smelled better or not. The smell of skunk was so powerful that it wasn't going to go away immediately, no matter how much hydrogen peroxide was rubbed on Dog.

Feebly, Dog licked Mason's hand, and then licked Brody's. He seemed to know that his two masters were trying to help.

"I'm sorry, Dog," Brody whispered, as if he had been the one who had suggested to Dog that it

would be a good idea to dash off after some strange black-and-white-striped animal.

Headlights appeared down the road, and Brody's parents' car pulled into the driveway, squealing to a stop.

"We tried to call!" Mason's mother said, leaping out of the backseat.

"*We* tried to call!" Mason shot back.

"Well, we got your message, and we're here now."

"It's good you washed him right away," Mason's dad said. "What are you washing him with?"

"Hydrogen peroxide, baking soda, some liquid detergent, and warm water," Brody replied.

"How on earth did you know what to do?" his mother asked.

"Nora told us," Brody said.

"Nora!" all the parents exclaimed in unison.

Nora stood, uncomfortable, as the parents continued to heap praise upon her. "I'm so glad the boys thought to call you!" "Talk about a quick mind in a crisis!" "I never would have thought of hydrogen peroxide!" "We're so lucky you were here!" If they were this impressed that she happened to remember one simple fact about hydrogen peroxide, what would they do when they read her published article about ants?

"Now, Mason," Mason's mother said, "even after this washing, he's still going to smell for a while. You know that, don't you?"

Mason looked puzzled. "What if he does?"

Mason's mother made her voice firm: "Dog needs to sleep in the garage tonight. I can't have him smelling up the entire house."

"No!" Mason and Brody cried together.

"It's cold in the garage!" Mason said.

"It's not even going to reach freezing tonight, and Dog has a nice warm fur coat," Mrs. Dixon pointed out.

"He'll think he's being punished," Brody said. "He'll think he did something wrong."

"Running after a skunk isn't the best or smartest thing he's ever done," Mason's father put in.

"Mom, he doesn't smell *that* bad," Mason insisted. "After a while, you get used to it."

"I have no intention of getting used to that smell in my house."

This time, both boys seemed to know they were defeated.

Then Brody's face brightened. It never took too long for Brody's face to brighten.

"Can we sleep in the garage, too?" he asked.

Even Mason's face brightened. And it took a lot to make Mason's face brighten. "So he'll know we still love him?" he joined in the pleading.

The four parents exchanged glances. The two sisters exchanged giggles.

"They do have sleeping bags," Mason's mom said slowly.

"And they can come inside if they get too cold," Brody's mom added.

"Hooray!" Brody said. "Dog, we're going to have a sleepover all night in the garage! You and Mason and me. And Nora! Nora, can you come, too?"

Nora hesitated. She was fond of Mason. She was fond of Brody. She was fond of Dog. But friendship had its limits.

"I think Nora has too much sense to want to sleep on a hard cement floor next to a stinking dog in an unheated garage in the middle of January," Mrs. Dixon said. "Am I correct, Nora?"

"I do need to get home," Nora said, trying to sound more reluctant than she actually felt.

Right this minute she was extra-glad that she had pets that didn't chase after skunks and get themselves banished to spending the night outside.

She took one last look at Brody and Mason. Both boys had laid their heads against Dog's broad back, one on each side, apparently not minding his dampness and smell.

Then she walked home under the golden streetlights to spend a cozy, warm evening indoors with her ants.

Ants also communicate by sound—they make tiny little squeaks. And they tap and stroke each other, too. I can't hear my ants squeaking. Can they hear me?

"So let's talk about persuasive speeches," Coach Joe said in the Monday-morning huddle. "What's the point of a persuasive speech?"

Nora hated when teachers asked questions that had super-obvious answers. She would feel silly raising her hand and saying, "The point of a persuasive speech is to try to persuade somebody of something so that they end up persuaded."

Emma never minded stating the obvious. "To persuade somebody," she said.

"Great!"

Emma gave a simpering little smile at Coach Joe's recognition of her brilliance.

"So what does that mean?" This time, fortunately, Coach Joe answered his own question. "It means that the person you're trying to persuade isn't yet persuaded, right? So what you're really trying to do in a persuasive speech is to change someone's mind. The audience for your speech is someone who isn't already rooting for your team. You want to make new fans, not play to the same fans you've had all season."

"You're never going to change some people's minds," Mason said. If Emma was the master of stating the obvious, Mason was the master of stating the negative.

"True," Coach Joe said. "You're completely right, Mason. Some people are just never going to be convinced by any challenge to what they already think. Patrick Henry and Thomas Paine, two of the best persuasive-speech writers of the American Revolution, knew they were never going to convince King George the Third or die-hard British loyalists. So who were they trying to convince?"

Nora raised her hand this time. "People who

hadn't made up their minds yet. People who were torn between both sides."

"Exactly. So maybe I misspoke earlier. The goal isn't so much to change someone's mind; that can be pretty tough, as our friend Mason pointed out. The goal of a persuasive speech is to help someone make up her mind. But that means speaking to the part of her mind that is tempted to favor the other side."

Some of the kids in the huddle had tuned out. Emma was fiddling with her charm bracelet, a silver chain hung with lots of little silver cats in different poses. Dunk, still made to sit right next to Coach Joe, appeared to be sleeping. Dunk's idea of persuading somebody would be threatening to sic his awful dog, Wolf, on them if they didn't give in.

"So," Coach Joe said, clearly realizing that he was losing half his team, "step one in writing a persuasive speech is figuring out your subject. But step two is equally important: figuring out your audience. Huddle dismissed. Back to your seats. You can talk quietly to your pod mates about your ideas. Just remember to ask: Who would be disagreeing with me? And why?"

Nora sat in a six-desk pod this month with Brody, Emma, and three other boys she didn't know very well. Coach Joe liked to move kids around. He called it changing the lineup. Poor Mason and Amy were currently in a pod with Dunk.

"So what do you want to write your persuasive speech about?" Nora asked. Someone needed to take charge of pod discussions, and that someone usually turned out to be her. At least it was easier to lead a discussion than it was to de-skunk a dog.

"I don't know," Jack said.

"I don't know," Nahil said.

"I don't know," Austin said.

Or maybe de-skunking a dog was easier.

"I know what I'm going to write about," Brody volunteered. "Mine is going to be great! It's going to be terrific! If people had only heard my speech in 1775, the whole course of history would have been different!"

Nora knew Brody well enough to know that he wasn't really bragging, however braggy he sounded. It was just his way of being enthusiastic. It wasn't bragging if Dog wagged his tail so hard it practically knocked someone over.

"Do you want to know what I'm going to write about?" Brody asked the others.

"No," Jack, Nahil, and Austin said in unison.

"Sure," Nora and Emma said at the same time.

Brody evidently preferred to listen to Nora and Emma.

"I'm going to persuade the colonists and the British *not* to have a war! To work out their differences in a peaceful way! If the British would just lower taxes and not tax things the colonists really love, like tea, the colonists wouldn't want to revolt, and the British could keep their colonies and get at least *some* tax money from them, which is better than none. Right? And nobody would die, which is even better. Right? And today we'd all be singing 'God Save the Queen' *and* 'My Country, 'Tis of Thee,' which would be perfect, because they both have the same tune anyway."

Brody's face was lit up with excitement. Nora could tell that he was ready to write his acceptance speech for the Nobel Peace Prize.

"I like it," Emma said.

Emma usually liked anything any boy wanted her to like, unless it was a boy she *really* liked, such as Dunk, and then she had to make a big show of pretending to hate it.

Brody's eyes sparkled from Emma's praise. Nora could tell he was waiting for her to praise him, too.

"Well," she said slowly, "preventing war is definitely a good thing to do. But don't you think the colonists already tried to make persuasive speeches to get their demands met? They didn't start out planning to go to war. War was their last resort, wasn't it?"

"Of course they tried," Brody agreed. "But I'm going to try harder. I'm going to try better."

"What are *you* going to write about?" Nora asked Emma.

"I'm going to write about"—Emma had raised her voice, clearly so that the people in the next pod would be able to hear her—"how cats are better than dogs."

Dunk got up from his pod and walked over to theirs.

"Oh yeah?" he said.

Emma giggled.

Dunk leaned in closer. "Well, I just decided what *I'm* going to write about."

Nora could tell that Dunk was relieved to have any idea at all.

"I'm going to write about how dogs are better than cats."

Emma giggled again.

"Dunk, back to your seat," Coach Joe called out.

"What do you think of my idea?" Emma asked her pod mates once Dunk had stomped away.

Jack, Nahil, and Austin shrugged.

"The problem with it is," Brody said, "that cats aren't better than dogs. Dunk is right." Certainly, this was the first time Brody had ever given Dunk credit for being right about anything. "My dog is the best animal in the whole world. No, in the whole universe."

"Nora, what do you think?" Emma asked, obviously hoping that the girls could stick together.

Nora copied her father and thought for a moment before answering.

"Actually, I don't think dogs are better *or* cats are better. Or pigs or porcupines. Animals aren't better or worse. They just are. That's like asking, 'Which are better, girls or boys?'"

"Girls!" Emma said, just as Jack, Nahil, and Austin said, "Boys!"

Brody didn't cast a vote on that one. He evidently didn't feel as strongly about boys versus girls as he did about dogs versus cats.

Nora shook her head. She should have realized that was a bad example.

"Anyway," she said, "it's good that our pod has a dog person and a cat person. It's like what Coach

Joe said. You have to try to persuade people who don't already agree with you. So Emma can try to persuade Brody."

Except that would be impossible.

"What about you, Nora?" Brody asked. "What are you going to write about?"

How ants are better than anything?

How people, such as Emma, should know more about science?

How there should be more famous women scientists, like Marie Curie? And, soon, Nora Alpers?

"I don't know," Nora admitted.

And then she realized that she sounded exactly like Jack, Nahil, and Austin.

Ants have been around for a long, long time. Scientists have found ant fossils in Europe that are more than 90 million years old. I hope they will be around for 90 million more years, at least.

8

After school on Monday, Nora went over to Mason's house to visit Dog and see how he was recovering from his encounter with the skunk.

"He doesn't smell at all anymore," Brody assured her as the three of them walked the few blocks to Mason's house. Mason's mom worked at home, editing an online knitting newsletter, so she was always there to welcome Mason and his friends.

"Well, he still smells a little bit," Mason corrected. "My parents looked it up on the Internet, and it's going to take a while for the skunk smell to go away completely."

"Like how long?" Nora asked.

"A couple of months," Mason admitted.

"So not very long at all!" Brody added.

When Dog ran up to greet them, tail wagging, Nora thought he smelled a *lot*.

"I know," Mason's mom said, in response to Nora's involuntarily wrinkled nose. "But I can't make him sleep in the garage forever. The three of you must be hungry. How about some roasted red pepper hummus and pita bread?"

"Hummus and pita sounds lovely," Nora said politely, even though she wasn't sure about the roasted red pepper part.

Brody, who liked all foods, nodded in happy agreement.

Mason had already gone to the pantry and grabbed a bag of Fig Newtons. Mason liked to eat the same foods over and over again: macaroni and cheese (from a box), peanut butter and jelly sandwiches, Cheerios (plain), and Fig Newtons (the original figgy kind).

"Fig Newtons, anyone?" he offered.

"Mason," his mother said, watching him put two Fig Newtons on a small plate and pour himself a glass of milk. "How do you know you aren't going to like hummus if you've never even tried it?"

"I don't have to try it to know it isn't Fig Newtons," Mason replied. "I don't have to try—what was that thing you tried to make me eat the other day? Baba something—baba smoosh?"

"Baba ghanoush," his mother said. "A delicious Middle Eastern dish of mashed eggplant and tahini."

"Baba whatever," Mason said. "I rest my case. I don't have to try mashed eggplant to know that it isn't macaroni and cheese. Even the word *eggplant* gives me the creeps. Doesn't it give you the creeps?" he asked Nora and Brody.

"Well, no," Nora said, even though she hated to side against Mason. Words weren't creepy; they were just words. Besides, lots of people thought things were creepy, like worms, spiders, snakes, and even ants, just because they didn't know anything about them. Mason's mother was right. Mason should give hummus and baba ghanoush a chance.

"Eggplant sounds like a plant that has eggs growing on it," Brody said. "That's weird, but not creepy weird, just funny weird."

"Mason," his mother said sadly, "what do I have to do to persuade you to at least *try* something new?"

Mason gave no reply. He just took another bite of Fig Newton.

Aside from smelling like burnt rubber, Dog was his old self, eager to go outside and dash after the battered tennis ball they threw for him in the yard. Even if he would never break any Guinness World Records for tennis ball fetching, he darted after the ball as quickly as if he were a dog with four legs.

"Guess what my mom is trying to make me do once basketball ends?" Mason asked. By his tone, Nora could tell he thought it was something extremely terrible.

"Voice lessons," Nora guessed. The music teacher at Plainfield Elementary was always telling Mason what a lovely voice he had, and Nora knew Mason lived in dread of being made to take voice lessons.

Mason shook his head.

"Joining some club that has Dunk in it?" Brody asked.

Nora tried to think of a club Dunk would join. She couldn't.

"No," Mason told them. "You'll never guess. No one could ever guess. So I'll have to tell you. My mother is trying to talk me into . . ."

He paused for effect.

"Figure skating! Ice skating! Doing fancy twirls and leaps and stuff on the ice!"

Nora couldn't help it. She burst out laughing. Brody doubled over, laughing, too.

Dog came up, panting, a ball in his mouth.

"At least Dog doesn't think it's funny," Mason said.

But Dog did look as if he were grinning as he dropped the ball at Mason's feet.

"If only," Mason said, "I could find a way to persuade my parents to stop trying to persuade *me* to do things!"

Monday evening, Nora's mother was off listening to an astronomy talk at the university, so Nora and her father were home all by themselves. All by themselves, except for her ants.

"I'm going to work on my ant experiments," Nora told her father as they cleared away the dishes after dinner.

"Do you need any help?" he asked.

"No!" Nora hadn't meant to sound so fierce, but it was one thing to have a footnote thanking Professor Neil Alpers for suggesting her line of research. It would be quite another thing if she had to thank Prof. Neil Alpers for helping with the research itself.

"Okay, sweetie" was all her father said. "If you need me, you know where to find me."

Nora had already cut a large sheet from a huge roll of butcher paper stored in the attic. She thought her ants would be more comfortable walking across paper than across the slippery, cold, bare bathtub. Now she laid the paper in the bottom of the tub, measured a square in the middle of it, and marked the square with bright blue chalk.

Gently, she extricated a dozen ants from her farm. Those would be enough ants to start with. She placed them in the middle of the square and set a small piece of cracker outside the square. Then she set the stopwatch on the tablet she had borrowed from her father.

The ants walked about. In two minutes and twenty-three seconds, the first ant reached the chalk line on one edge of the square, the edge farthest from the cracker.

Then the ant stopped.

Another ant followed her. (Nora knew they were

both female ants, because all worker ants are fe-males.)

That ant stopped, too.

Nora stared. Ants didn't seem to want to cross a line made of chalk! How could they even know there was a line there? Why would they care? They must have smelled the chalk or felt the chalk dust with their feet.

As Nora continued to watch, two other ants stopped short their wanderings at a different edge of the square, also reluctant to walk across the chalk line.

She drew in her breath. This was a pattern! This was a real, observable, scientific result!

But three other ants, which had reached the edge of the chalk square closest to the cracker, hesitated, and then did cross over the line, taking a direct path to the cracker.

Ants were willing to cross the chalk line if there was food on the other side!

Wishing she had remembered to bring her parents' video camera up to the bathroom, Nora contented herself with watching and timing. Sir Isaac Newton hadn't had a video camera to record the falling apple. He had just watched it fall.

For the next hour, Nora sat on the rim of the bathtub, completely still, blissfully watching, measuring, and timing her ants.

There are about 12,500 species of ants known to science. Maybe I will discover some new ant species someday. I think I already made a huge, important ant discovery today!

9

On Tuesday, Emma wore a pink sweater with a fluffy white cat on it to school. The cat wasn't flat; it poofed out of the sweater with soft, fuzzy white yarn. An actual small plaid ribbon perched on top of its head.

The girls at lunch squealed with rapture.

"It looks so real!" Bethy said. "Can I pat its fur?"

"If your hands are clean," Emma told her. "Not if you've been eating."

"I haven't even touched my tuna melt yet," Bethy promised.

With one gentle finger, she stroked the fur of Emma's sweater cat.

"It's so soft!" she exclaimed.

"Can I touch it?" Elise asked.

"Me, too!" chimed in Tamara. Even Amy gave the sweater an admiring smile.

Nora made sure to take a first bite of her tuna melt sandwich so that her hands wouldn't meet Emma's cat-petting standard.

"Sorry," she mumbled, with her mouth full. "I was starving!"

"It's soooo cute," Amy admitted. "Her ribbon even has sparkles on it."

"Mega-cute," Elise agreed. "Look! She has real whiskers!"

"The cutest cat in the world!" Tamara gushed.

The sudden frosty look on Emma's face let Tamara know that her praise of the sweater cat had gone too far.

"Except for Precious Cupcake, of course," Tamara hastily corrected herself. "Precious Cupcake is the cutest *real* cat in the world. This is the cutest *cat on a sweater* in the world."

Emma's smile returned.

"I know," she said.

Nora chomped down on another bite of tuna melt. She wouldn't have minded all the fuss over Emma's cat sweater if she hadn't known how differently the girls—well, except for Amy—would have reacted if she had worn a pink sweater covered with little black ants.

"Ewww!"

"Gross!"

"They look so real!"

Screams from Emma. A stampede away from the table.

Maybe Nora should defy the code of the Plainfield Elementary animal kingdom and go sit with Mason and Brody and their other friends. But she knew she wouldn't; she couldn't. Animal kingdom behavior wasn't that easy to change, even if a human animal really wanted to change it.

Nora took a big swig of milk to force down a bite of sandwich she was having trouble swallowing.

On Wednesday, Dunk wore a T-shirt that said I HATE CATS. Beneath the slogan was a big red circle crossing out the silhouette of a cat. The T-shirt looked brand-new, unlike Dunk's usual clothes, which bore stubborn stains of catsup, mustard, and whatever his horrid dog, Wolf, had rolled in lately.

As soon as Dunk yanked off his jacket in the cubby room, Emma's eyes widened.

"Ooh!" she seethed, jabbing him in the chest. Her rage today seemed real to Nora rather than pretend. You could sound mad even if you weren't really angry. It would be a lot harder to make your cheeks flush on demand.

Dunk grinned.

Other boys whooped and hollered and thumped him on the back.

Emma's friends formed a protective circle around her as Nora stood watching. Nora had no interest in taking sides in the war between cat lovers and dog lovers in Coach Joe's class. But if she were to take sides, right now she'd side with Emma. It was one thing to love your own kind of pet. It was another to hate someone else's kind of pet.

When Dunk tried to sit next to Emma in Coach Joe's huddle, even before Coach Joe could make Dunk move, Emma got up and flounced away.

Dunk gave his usual donkey-like guffaw.

He plainly didn't get the difference between Emma's fake rage and her real rage.

But Nora did.

After school, Nora hung out with Amy. The two girls went for a walk with Amy's two dogs, Nora walking Amy's big dog, Woofer, on one leash while Amy walked her little dog, Tweeter, on another. It was considerate of Amy to have a dog for each of them.

Amy had a cat for each friend, too. Earlier in the afternoon, Mush Ball had been cuddling on Nora's lap while Snookers had been snuggling with Amy.

Amy even had a rabbit for each of them out in a hutch in her backyard, and a pair of parakeets in a cage in her dining room.

But there was one pet Amy didn't have, the best pet of all: ants.

"So which do *you* think is better, dogs or cats?" Nora asked, knowing which answer she hoped Amy would give.

"Neither! I mean, why do we have to take sides? Dogs are better at being dogs, and cats are better at being cats."

Nora couldn't have said it better herself.

Woofer stopped to smell something buried under the new snow. Nora had read that a dog's sense of smell was thousands of times better than a human's. Even though a dog brain was only one-tenth the size of a human brain, the smelling part of its brain was forty times larger.

For a moment, Nora envied Amy for having so many different animals she could study, so many notebooks' worth of fascinating facts. But maybe it was better to study one subject in greater depth. Her mother was an expert on Saturn, not Saturn *and* Jupiter *and* Mars. It was enough to be an expert on Saturn—and not even on all of Saturn, just on its rings.

As they walked on, Amy said, "I thought I'd write my persuasive speech about how people shouldn't dress up their pets in costumes. Pets hate costumes! And it's almost like we're making fun of them, laughing at how ridiculous they look. You know what I mean?"

Nora certainly did.

"But then I thought . . . well, you know . . ."

"Emma," Nora said.

"She wouldn't like it."

That was an understatement.

"But I feel sorry for Precious Cupcake sometimes, I really do," Amy said.

"Me, too," Nora said.

Woofer stopped to sniff at a tree. Tweeter strained at his leash to dart after a squirrel. And then the two girls walked on.

That evening, Nora worked on writing her ant article. She thought of a catchy title for it: "The Ants Go Marching—Until They Reach the Chalk Line!" Maybe the editors would think that was an attention-getting title. She would certainly want to read an article with that title.

She had repeated the same experiment three times on Monday night and gotten the same results. That was important in science. You didn't know if your results were real, and not just a fluke, unless you got the same results over and over again. So she put that in her article, too. And she made a chart of all her measurements: how long it had taken the ants to reach the perimeter of the square, how long it had taken them to cross the chalk line to reach the cracker.

This was going to be the best ant article ever!

In school on Thursday, Dunk wore his I HATE CATS T-shirt again, apparently not noticing that it hadn't gotten the results he wanted on Wednesday. Nora was struck by how much more quickly her ants were willing to change their behavior when a strategy wasn't working.

Emma wasn't wearing her fuzzy-cat sweater, but she had on her cat necklace *and* a cat charm bracelet. She spent most of the day, as far as Nora could tell, fiddling with them. Lunchtime was non-stop cat videos. The other girls seemed a bit worn out with gushing.

"I think we saw that one already," Amy said.

"My mother said I could have an ice-skating party for my birthday," Tamara said, daring to change the subject.

Nora couldn't help wondering if Mason's mother had signed him up for ice-skating lessons yet.

"I love ice skating!" Elise said.

"Me, too!" said Bethy.

"Speaking of ice skating, I have a video of Precious Cupcake outside in the snow," Emma said. "Let me see if I can find it."

But the other girls just kept on talking about how much fun an ice-skating party would be, especially if they could wear special ice-skating skirts and send invitations cut out in the shape of ice skates.

At home that afternoon, Nora sat down at the computer in the family room to try to type her ant article. A real science journal would expect articles to be typed, not written out by hand. She didn't have a computer of her own, but her parents let her use the computer and printer on the desk in the family room whenever she wanted. Luckily, her mother made her father keep all of his mess contained in his own office, so the family room desk was always an invitingly neat place for Nora to work.

If only she were a faster typist. Coach Joe's class went to the computer lab twice a week for keyboarding, but Nora still typed so slowly and made so many mistakes. When she heard her parents typing, their fingers flew over the keys with amazing speed, especially her father's. He could probably be in the *Guinness World Records* book for fastest typing.

Sitting at the computer, Nora created a new file—*Nora ant article*—and typed in her first sentence: "Is there aynthing in the wrld more fscinatnig than ants?"

Coach Joe liked them to begin with a question to engage the reader. She hoped the editors of a grown-up science journal would like the same thing.

Reading her sentence over, she saw four mistakes in it. It took her another two minutes to correct them: "Is there anything in the world more fascinating than ants?"

Maybe she could ask her father to type the article for her. It wasn't very long. He could probably type it in five minutes. It would take her more like five hours. No, not five hours. Nora wasn't one for dramatic exaggeration. But it would take her a frustrating amount of time. It wouldn't be cheating if he typed it for her so long as she added that to her thank-you footnote:

"I would like to thank Professor Neil Alpers for suggesting this line of research and for typing this article for me."

She saved her one completed sentence on the computer—she certainly didn't want to have to type the whole thing over again—and wandered up to her dad's messy office. She hadn't told either of her parents yet about her publication plan. The thought of telling them made her feel shy for some reason. They had always supported her love of science. How could they not, given that they were both scientists themselves? But they might say, "Oh, honey, I don't think a real grown-up journal is going to want an ant article by a ten-year-old."

Would a real grown-up science journal want an ant article by a ten-year-old?

Nora felt a twinge of doubt.

Maybe her first sentence didn't sound scientific enough. Coach Joe's advice might not apply to scientific articles; maybe those articles weren't supposed to begin with a question. Their readers were probably already so wild to learn about science that they wanted to jump right in and skip the beginning stuff altogether.

And she didn't even know of any ant journals where she could send her article. How would she know which ant journals were the best?

Her father was hunched over his computer, typing at his usual Guinness World Record speed.

"What's up?" he asked, swirling toward her in his big swivel chair.

"Nothing." She moved a pile of journals from his couch to the floor so that she could sit down, careful to keep them all in order. Her father claimed that even though his office looked like a mess, he knew exactly where everything was.

The top journal in the pile was called *Nature*.

Nature was a huge subject. It would include every single thing in the natural world. Including ants.

Nora picked it up and thumbed through it. She saw lots of graphs. She'd have to be sure to put graphs in her article. Luckily, she already knew how to make graphs on the computer. There were lots of footnotes, too, numbered stuff in little type at the bottom of each page. At least she'd have one footnote, the thank-you to Professor Alpers. One footnote was better than nothing.

"Did you ever have an article in this one?" she asked her dad.

"Once. That's a tough one to get in, because it has so many different kinds of science in it."

"How did they know to pick you? Did they already know how smart you are?"

He chuckled. "Hardly. They send each article off to experts in the field. The experts review it blind. That means without knowing who wrote it, so they won't be influenced by anything except by how good the science is."

Nora liked that part. The ant experts who read her article wouldn't know that she was only ten. They would just care about how much she knew about ants.

"So anybody could publish an article here if it was good enough?" she persisted.

Her father nodded.

"Even a kid?"

To her great disappointment, he didn't give her an encouraging grin.

"Well . . ."

"Why not a kid?" Nora demanded.

"Well, there's no reason why a person's age in

itself should make a difference," he said slowly. "But I have to say, it's exceedingly unlikely that a child would be able to compete against adult scientists with their doctorate degrees and fancy labs."

Nora lifted her chin.

Did any of those adult scientists, with their doctorate degrees and fancy labs, love ants the way she did?

And that girl in the record book, Emily Rosa: she hadn't had a doctorate degree or a fancy lab, and she was only a year older than Nora.

"Is there anything you came in to ask me?" her father asked, glancing over at his computer screen as if he wanted to get back to work.

"No," Nora said. "Can I borrow this?" She held up the copy of *Nature*.

"Sure."

Nora thought he looked amused. Had he figured out that she was planning to send her ant article off to *Nature* as soon as she finished typing it? Now she was definitely going to type it all by herself, without help from any grown-up. She was never going to ask for help from a grown-up on anything ever again!

Did her father think she was *funny*?

Even worse, did he think she was *cute*?

Without another word, Nora stalked out of his office and shut the door.

Let her father try to hide a smile! She was going to show Professor Neil Alpers just what a ten-year-old ant-loving scientist could do.

Ants differ enormously in size. An entire colony of the smallest ants could fit inside the head of one of the most giant ants! But just because some ants are smaller, that doesn't make them any less important.

10

It took Nora two hours to type her article. When she printed it out, it was only four pages, including the graphs, which were in color.

Was that too short for a real grown-up article?

No, she decided. What mattered in science were your experiment and what it proved: your data. You didn't need to go on and on about it for pages, just repeating the same points over and over.

She looked again at her graphs.

Ants busy in their tunnels were the most beautiful thing in the world. But the second-most beautiful thing was graphs about ants, printed in color!

She probably needed to write a letter to go with the article. The letter didn't have to be long, either. This was a business letter, not a friendly letter, so she used the format Coach Joe had taught them for business letters. She was too worn out from typing the article to type the letter, too. But she wrote it in cursive, even though she wasn't very good at cursive. Cursive looked more grown-up and business-like than printing.

Dear Sir or Madam:
　Here is the article I wrote about my research into ants.
　I hope you want to publish it.
　　　　　　Sincerely,
　　　　　　Nora Alpers

She found an envelope in the desk drawer and wrote the address on it. Her parents kept a roll of stamps in the drawer, too. They were both great believers in writing old-fashioned letters, the kind you wrote by hand and sent in the mail, so they had told her she could help herself to stamps whenever she needed one.

"I'm going for a walk!" she called upstairs to them.

Faintly, her mother's voice called back, "Dinner in half an hour!"

The closest mailbox was in front of the post office, just three blocks away, in the other direction from where Amy lived. Nora could have put her letter for pickup in the mailbox at home, but then her parents might see it. She wasn't going to tell them anything until the issue with the published article came in the mail. Even then she wasn't going to *tell* them. She'd let them find out on their own.

The new issue would arrive in the mail.

Her father would flip through it before sticking it on the top of one of the huge piles of paper in his office.

His eyes would fall on a familiar name.

He'd stare at it, unable to believe what he saw.

"Nora!" he'd holler. "Nora, is this *you*? Janine, come see what our daughter just did!"

These pleasant thoughts occupied Nora all the way to the post office. Now she stood in front of the mailbox, her letter clutched tightly in her hand.

She wasn't a superstitious person. She didn't believe in magic or luck or special charms to make things happen. But she still gave her envelope one little kiss—not for luck, really, just to wish it success on its way.

She slipped it into the mail slot and hugged herself with happiness.

At lunch on Friday, Emma started talking as soon as all the girls had sat down. She always talked more than everybody else put together, but today she obviously had something extra-important to share.

"Over winter break, my mother took me and my sister to the Brown Palace Hotel in Denver for high tea. *High tea* means extra-fancy tea. You don't just have tea; you also have scones—these yummy little biscuit things—with cream and jam. And itty-bitty cucumber sandwiches—I know that sounds weird, but they're ultra-British, and they're good, too. They really are, with the crusts cut off to make them even fancier. Plus lots of little frosted cakes. And everyone was all dressed up—with hats! And a lady wearing a long dress was playing beautiful music on a harp. It was the best time I ever had in my life."

Nora was surprised that the best time Emma ever had in her life was a time Precious Cupcake hadn't even been there.

"There was one thing missing, of course," Emma said then.

Of course.

"Precious Cupcake couldn't come with me, because they don't allow pets at their high tea. *Any* pets. So . . ."

Emma paused. When all eyes were on her, she continued.

"I'm going to have my own high tea just for Precious Cupcake and a few of my best friends. It's going to be this Sunday afternoon from three to five. I know this is short notice, but can you all come? Say yes!"

"Yes!" chorused Bethy, Elise, Tamara, and Amy. A high tea like the one at the Brown Palace Hotel was even more exciting than an ice-skating party.

"Nora, you're invited, too," Emma said, as if Nora might be hesitating because she wasn't sure if she was a best-enough best friend to be included in such a select invitation.

Nora didn't particularly want to eat cucumber sandwiches with Emma's cat. But she didn't want to hurt Emma's feelings, either, especially since Dunk was wearing his now grubby and stained I HATE CATS T-shirt for the third day in a row. Emma, who usually never wore the same outfit twice in a month, was wearing her fluffy-cat sweater for the second time that week.

"Thank you," Nora said. "I'd love to."

Coach Joe let kids bring in treats on their birthdays. Today was the birthday of one of Brody's friends, Sheng. So Sheng's mother had brought in cupcakes.

When the school day was almost over, Sheng went around setting paper plates with cupcakes on them on everybody's desks.

Emma beamed as if Sheng had chosen to bring cupcakes in honor of Precious Cupcake. "Thank you," she told him, with the kind of smile she used to give to Dunk. "I love cupcakes."

She turned toward Nora. "We'll be having mini-cupcakes at the high tea in addition to the scones and cucumber sandwiches. Of course!"

"That will be nice," Nora said politely.

"Cupcakes are awesome," Brody agreed, his face already dabbed with frosting.

Out of the corner of her eye, Nora saw Dunk heading toward their pod.

Emma had been snubbing Dunk all week. No

giggles when he told her that Wolf could eat Precious Cupcake for breakfast. No girly squeals when he jostled her tray in the lunch line and slopped tomato soup all over her grilled cheese sandwich. No one could do frosty disdain better than Emma Averill, Nora had to give her that.

But Dunk still didn't seem to get it. The more Emma snubbed him, the harder he tried to impress her by horsing around with the other boys and saying mean things about cats in general and Precious Cupcake in particular.

Now he approached, cupcake in hand.

"*Precious Cupcake* is a dumb name for a cat," Dunk said, as a friendly opening.

Nora couldn't disagree with that.

He grinned at Emma hopefully, plainly expecting that she would finally break down and giggle again as in days of yore.

She didn't.

Nor did she say, "*Wolf* is a dumb name for a dog." Or: "*Dunk* is a dumb name for a boy."

She just looked through Dunk as if he weren't even there.

Dunk flushed a dull red.

"Well, here's a cupcake for *that* dumb cat," he said.

He thrust his cupcake toward Emma's cat sweater. Emma shrieked, not a happy shriek but the same terrified shriek she had given at the sight of Nora's ant farm.

Startled, Dunk dropped the cupcake. It landed, frosting side down, on Emma's favorite flouncy skirt.

"I hate you, Dunk!" Emma burst into tears just as Coach Joe came over to their pod, saying, "Team, team. What's going on?"

At least the cupcake hadn't gotten on Emma's sweater cat, the cat that nobody was allowed to touch without proof of clean hands.

But that was little consolation as Emma sat crying and Dunk looked as if he was about to cry, too.

Male ants live a much shorter time than females—only a few weeks or months. Most of them do no work at all! I'm not saying this to be critical of boy ants. This is just a fact.

Nora wore a dress to Emma's high tea for Precious Cupcake, but she drew the line at a hat. The only hats she owned were warm stocking caps for the winter and canvas hats with sun visors for the summer, plus one old-fashioned sunbonnet her parents had bought her at a crafts fair. She tried the sunbonnet on just to see how it looked with her dress, but then she took it off again. It made her look like a pioneer girl from *Little House on the Prairie,* not a typical guest at an elegant tea party. Of course, Precious Cupcake wasn't going to look like a typical guest at an elegant tea party, either.

"My, don't you look pretty," her mother commented as Nora came downstairs right before the party.

Nora made a face. Whenever she wore a dress, people always made a point of telling her that she looked pretty.

Had people ever told Marie Curie, discoverer of radium, that she looked pretty?

Did they tell Jane Goodall, the world's foremost expert on chimpanzees, that she looked pretty?

Nora greatly doubted it.

Her mother drove her to Emma's house.

"How long do you think it would take a piece of mail to get from Colorado to New York?" Nora asked her mother. She had mailed her ant article to *Nature* on Thursday, and now it was Sunday.

"Two days?" her mother guessed. "Why?"

"I was just wondering," Nora said.

"That's one of the things I love most about you," her mother told her. "You're always wondering about something."

If Nora's mother was right, her ant article would have arrived yesterday, Saturday. The editors at

Nature probably didn't work on the weekend. Or maybe they did? Her scientist parents worked as hard on weekends as they did during the week. Say they got it Saturday and sent it off right away to the big ant expert. The ant expert would get it on—Tuesday? And read it on Wednesday. And send the review off on Thursday. The editors would get the review back on Saturday.

There was no way she was going to hear anything in less than a week. More likely two or even three, in case the ant expert was busy with other things, like grading exams for his ant students or writing ant papers of his own.

His or *her* own.

"How are you supposed to act at a fancy tea party?" Nora asked her mother as they pulled into Emma's long, curved driveway.

"Actually," her mother said, "I don't believe I've ever been to a fancy tea party. You'll have to tell *me* when you get home. Just follow Emma's lead."

Well, if Nora followed Emma's lead, she'd be spending most of the tea party fussing over Precious Cupcake.

"Have fun!" her mother told her.

"I'll try," Nora replied.

The first thing Nora noticed, when she caught a glimpse of the other guests through the double doors leading into Emma's dining room, was that they were all wearing hats. The hats looked like Easter bonnets, not that Nora had ever seen an Easter bonnet in real life. Their dresses were covered with lace, ruffles, and bows.

Nora's own dress was plain and simple. It looked sporty, not poofy, more like a dress you could play basketball in, if anybody ever played basketball wearing a dress. More like a dress an ant scientist would wear.

Emma looked worried as she took Nora's coat.

"Would you like to borrow a hat?" she asked in a low voice, so the girls in the other room wouldn't hear. "I have a hat that would look great with your dress. Kind of, you know, dress it up a bit?"

Nora hesitated. She'd feel strange, un-Nora-like, if she borrowed Emma's hat. But she already felt un-Nora-like being at Emma's tea party in the first place. And her mother *had* told her to follow Emma's lead.

"Sure," Nora said.

Emma darted upstairs and returned a moment later with a hat for Nora. The hat was made of lavender straw, with a huge, floppy yellow flower on one side, as big as a sunflower, but definitely not a sunflower. Nora was pretty sure it was a flower unknown to botanists, a flower found nowhere in the natural world.

Ridiculous hat perched bravely on her head, Nora caught a glimpse of herself in the small, round mirror on the wall leading to the dining room.

Oh well.

Emma's mother appeared, as dressed up as her daughter, also wearing a hat.

"Why, Nora," she said. "Don't you look pretty!"

Nora forced herself to smile.

"I love your hat! I believe Emma has one almost exactly like it. That yellow flower is just darling!"

Nora made her smile even wider.

Emma's dining room table was covered with a long white tablecloth. Seven places were set with strawberry-patterned plates and matching teacups and saucers. Nora saw that each place was marked with a flowered name card written in a graceful cursive that had to have been done by Emma's mother.

Nora found hers: Miss Nora Alpers.

As the six girls took their seats, Nora saw that one seat was still empty—the seat at her left—where the chair was piled high with cushions.

Its name card read: Miss Precious Cupcake.

"Where *is* Precious Cupcake?" Bethy asked. "Doesn't she know the whole party is for *her*?"

"The guest of honor always arrives *last*," Emma informed Bethy.

"Oh," Bethy said. "I didn't know."

As if on cue, Emma's older sister, wearing a black dress with a frilly white apron and matching frilly white cap, entered, cradling Precious Cupcake in her arms. Nora had thought Precious Cupcake might be wearing the same pink cape and silver tiara she had displayed in the "Princess Precious" cat video, but the cat had a new outfit Nora had never seen before. This time, it was an actual dress, just like a girl's dress, pink with embroidered strawberries all over it and a pink satiny ribbon tied around it. The outfit was topped off by a hat with a large yellow flower that looked to be the same genus and species as the flower on Nora's hat.

A hush fell over the guests at the table.

Then:

"Ooh!"

"Aww!"

"She's sooooo cute!"

"She's the cutest ever!"

Nora widened her already wide smile.

"Nora," Elise said, "her flower looks just like yours!"

"It does!" Tamara agreed.

"You're the Precious Cupcake twins!" Bethy said.

Nora's face was starting to ache from smiling.

Emma's sister set Precious Cupcake on the chair of honor. Nora expected the cat to leap away and scurry for shelter. But Precious Cupcake stayed at her royal post as if she attended fancy tea parties all the time and knew exactly how to behave.

Maybe Nora could just follow the cat's lead now.

"May I pour you some tea?" Emma asked, gesturing toward the silver teapot her mother had just placed on the table.

"Yes, please!" came a chorus of replies.

"Let me help with the pouring," Emma's mother offered. "The tea is very hot. Girls, I hope you all like strawberry herbal tea."

117

"Strawberry, to match the strawberries on the plates," Emma explained. "And the strawberries on Precious Cupcake's dress."

Emma's sister was serving as party waitress. Her little frilly apron and cap must be her waitress costume. She now appeared carrying two silver trays, one balanced on each hand.

"Cucumber sandwiches and scones," Emma announced. "There's clotted cream—that's the white stuff in the little bowl—and lemon curd—that's the yellow stuff—and raspberry preserves—that's a fancy word for jam. Oh, that reminds me. We all need to start talking in a fancy way."

"Like people in the olden days?" Elise asked. "Like, instead of saying, *I would like some more tea*, say, *I would liketh some more tea*."

For the first time since her guests had arrived, Emma looked unsure. "Well, maybe."

"And say *thee* and *thou*," Elise added. She was the biggest reader of any of the girls at the table, except for Nora. But Nora didn't tend to read books about people who said *thee* and *thou*. "Would thou pourest me some tea?" Elise said, as an example to show the other girls.

Emma plainly didn't like having anything at her

tea party dictated by someone else. "Well, I don't think we need to go *that* far," she said.

"How about, thou *can* talketh that way, but thou doesn't *have* to," Tamara suggested.

"Okay then," Emma agreed grudgingly. "That sounds—I mean, that soundeth—good."

Emma's sister arrived with yet another silver tray, this one filled with tiny pink-frosted cupcakes, each one topped with a sliver of real strawberry.

"Emma, I loveth this tea party!" Elise said.

"I'm glad you love it," Emma said. "I mean, that thou loveth it."

Nora helped herself to a cucumber sandwich, scone, and cupcake. She tried a bite of scone with clotted cream and raspberry preserves. It was delicious. She was relieved to see that Precious Cupcake was served different, species-appropriate treats: a dollop of wet cat food on a strawberry-patterned saucer, and part of what smelled like an anchovy.

"So, Emma," Bethy said. "Tell us. Does thou hatest Dunk now?"

Emma's face darkened. "I do! I do hateth him. Because he hateth Precious Cupcake, and he almost ruineth my favorite sweater."

"I hate *all* boys," Elise declared. "What about the rest of you? Do you hateth all boys, too?"

Nora was glad to see that *thou* had apparently been dropped from the conversation. She couldn't imagine how Elise could have asked that same question with *thou* in it. *What about the rest of thous? Do thous hateth all boys, too?* Even though she hadn't read any books with *thee* and *thou* in them, she knew that couldn't possibly be right.

"Yes!" the other girls all answered.

"What about you, Nora?" Bethy asked. "Do you hate all boys, too?"

Even to follow Emma's lead, Nora couldn't lie. "No. I like Mason. I like Brody. It doesn't make sense to hate *all* boys or *all* dogs or *all* cats or *all* of anything."

"So do you *like* like Mason? Or *like* like Brody?" Elise persisted. "If I didn't hate all boys, I might not hate Brody."

Nora didn't feel like talking anymore about hating or *like* liking boys. But Emma wasn't going to let Elise's question drop.

"So do you, Nora? *Like* like Mason or Brody?"

"No."

Desperately, Nora looked around for something else to talk about besides boys or Precious Cupcake, who, she saw, was still sitting nicely in her place, the perfect guest in every respect.

Except for one.

Precious Cupcake was just now swallowing the pink ribbon from her pink cat dress.

"Emma!" Nora cried. "Precious Cupcake!"

All eyes turned to the cat as the last tip of pink ribbon disappeared down her throat.

Some ants can snap their jaws shut so fast that it's one of the fastest body-part movements ever recorded in the animal kingdom. Precious Cupcake didn't swallow her ribbon that fast. But she definitely swallowed it faster than I could think to stop her.

12

That was the end of high tea.

Emma sat sobbing, hugging Precious Cupcake even as she kept crying, "Bad cat! Bad cat!" Emma's mother called the vet, and they said to take Precious Cupcake to urgent veterinary care because a long swallowed ribbon could cause a blockage in a cat's intestines. The vet said that Precious Cupcake might need surgery. Emma sobbed even harder.

"Oh, Precious Cupcake, how could you?" she moaned.

All the girls, including Nora, crowded around

Emma to try to comfort her, but Emma couldn't be comforted.

Emma's mother loaded a loudly meowing Precious Cupcake into the cat carrier. Nora could see that it had what looked like a velvet cushion inside. Then Emma and her mother left for the vet. Emma's sister, still in her lacy waitress apron and cap, stayed while the guests called their parents for rides home. It was only at the last minute that Nora remembered that she was still wearing Emma's flowered hat. She set it on the front hall table, her head free at last.

"So how was it?" her mother asked in the car on the way home. "Except for poor Precious Cupcake, of course."

"It was okay." The scone had been tasty, even though Nora hadn't been able to finish it with all the commotion over Cupcake's catastrophe. "I didn't really liketh it, but I didn't hateth it, either."

"Liketh? Hateth?"

"*That's* what people do at fancy tea parties," Nora told her. "They talk in a fancy way."

"Oh," her mother said. "Well, now we know."

Emma's vet decided that Precious Cupcake should be observed for twenty-four hours to see if the ribbon "emerges from the other end." That was what Emma told the girls at lunch on Monday.

"Emerges from the other end?" Elise asked.

"You know," Amy said, with veterinary authority. "The *other* end."

"Ewww!" said Tamara.

"Gross!" said Bethy.

"Is someone going to have to *check*?" Elise wanted to know. "Ick!"

Emma plainly didn't like having the words *ewww, gross,* and *ick* applied in any way to Precious Cupcake. She drew herself up erect and glared at her friends.

Nora didn't understand how the other girls could be so grossed out by an ordinary bodily function they themselves performed every day. Mason and Brody cleaned up after Dog. Emma probably scooped out the litter box, or someone in her family did. Nora's own ants carefully dealt with their waste, keeping it separate in a special area of the ant farm. What was *ewww, gross,* or *ick* about it?

"It's better than making her have surgery," Nora pointed out, trying to turn the conversation in a sensible direction. Amy nodded in agreement.

But the cries of *ewww, gross,* and *ick* had already drawn Dunk to their table, an eager glint in his eye. If there was anyone who was an expert in things that could be described in that way, it was Dunk.

"What happened?" he asked, hopeful. "What's gross?"

"Don't tell him," Emma commanded.

But Bethy couldn't resist. "Precious Cupcake swallowed a ribbon, and now Emma has to wait and see if it—well—if it—you know—comes out the other end."

"If she *poops* it out?" Dunk practically shouted. He burst into the loudest guffaws Nora had heard from him yet.

Emma turned on him with a look of the fiercest rage Nora had seen from her yet.

"My cat might have to have an operation!" she spat out. "My cat might die!"

Nora thought Emma was exaggerating just a bit, for effect.

"Swallowing a ribbon can be fatal to cats! You think that's *funny*? If my cat dies, you're going to *laugh*?"

Poor Dunk, Nora thought. This was even worse than trying to smush his frosted cupcake onto Emma's cat sweater.

For the first time, Dunk seemed to get it.

"I don't want—" he stammered. "I just—I mean—poop is funny. Isn't it?"

All of the girls now stared at him with utter disdain.

Dunk's lower lip quivered. "I don't want your cat to die!" he blubbered.

Emma continued to freeze him with her stare, until finally Dunk slunk away back to his own table. Bethy put her arm around Emma's shaking shoulders.

"What if Precious Cupcake does die?" Emma whispered.

Elise's eyes glistened.

Tamara wiped away a tear.

Nora had had all she could take. "She's not going to die." She looked over at Amy, who nodded.

"How do you know?" Bethy shot back.

"I don't *know*," Nora said. "But it's very unlikely. Pets swallow things they shouldn't all the time. Usually those things pass right through them."

"That's right," Amy agreed. "And pets have operations all the time and come through them just fine."

But the other girls were obviously in the mood to be sad. Nora couldn't help but think it was all partly a show to make Dunk feel even worse than he did already.

She sighed and finished eating her ham and cheese sandwich. Someone had to stay calm, cool, and collected. And, as often as not, she was that someone.

At home that evening, Nora was curled up on the family room couch, busy at work on her persuasive speech, her ants beside her, busy with another ant funeral. A lot of them had been dying lately. Nora knew as well as anyone that a colony without a queen couldn't survive forever.

But she didn't let herself dwell on that unpleasant thought. She had to focus on her speech, which was due on Friday, just four days away.

She had decided to pull all of her ideas together and write about how more people should study science, especially girls. She had looked up statistics on what percentage of PhD degrees in science was awarded to women: not a very big one. If only more people studied science, more people would care about all the amazing creatures of the world, many of them endangered now by loss of habitat and climate change. If only more people, especially girls like Emma, studied science, they might even appreciate ants.

At seven-thirty, the phone rang. Nora picked it up.

The caller didn't identify herself, but Nora knew right away who it was and what the call was about.

It was a girl.

And the girl said, "It came out!"

So Nora had been correct, after all.

Precious Cupcake was going to be just fine.

One of the greatest perils ants face in nature is drought. I make sure to give my ants enough water so they are never thirsty. An experiment I'm not going to try: if I gave them part of a ribbon to eat, would they eat it?

13

Nora had already calculated that the soonest she could possibly hear from *Nature* about her ant article would be next week. And she could hear by next week only if the big ant expert dropped everything else, pounced upon her article, and read it right away.

But as soon as she got home from school on Wednesday, her father, who was working at home, handed her a letter.

"You got something from *Nature*," he said, looking puzzled. "How on earth would they have gotten your name and address? It doesn't look like a mass mailing, either. It looks like a letter sent just to you."

Stalling for time, Nora studied the envelope, addressed to Miss Nora Alpers.

Her father stood waiting for her to open it. Her parents would never open a piece of mail addressed to somebody else. They believed in privacy. But her father might as well have opened her letter, as he plainly planned on standing there until he found out what it said.

Well, she had been planning to tell him sooner or later. It might as well be sooner.

But today was too soon. Even the speediest ant expert couldn't possibly have had time to review her article yet.

"Aren't you going to open it?" her father said.

Nora picked up the fancy silver letter opener her parents kept on the front hall table and slid it under the flap of the envelope. She drew out the one sheet of paper inside. The paper was thick and fancy, with *Nature* printed at the top.

She started reading.

Dear Miss Alpers:

Thank you for sending us your article, "The Ants Go Marching—Until They Reach the Chalk Line!" We are impressed that you have such a serious scientific interest in ants at your age.

We are unable to publish this in Nature, but we hope you will send us other articles when you are older. We wish you all the best with your future career in science.

The letter was signed at the bottom with an illegible scrawl from the editor.

"So?" her father asked.

"They rejected it," Nora said in a small voice. "I wrote an article about my ants, and I sent it to them, and they said to try again when I'm *older*."

Nora didn't tell him that she had been trying to break the Guinness World Record for youngest person to publish an article in a grown-up science journal. That goal now seemed as ridiculous as Brody's thinking he could get Dog to hold the most tennis balls in his mouth or walk the longest distance with a glass of water on his head.

Who was she to think she could break a world record for anything?

"You sent an article to *Nature*?" her father asked, even though that was what she had already told him.

She handed him the letter so he could read it himself.

"I don't think they even showed it to the big ant expert," she whispered.

"What big ant expert?"

"*You* know. You said they send the articles off to big experts. But I think they just wrote me back right away. Because I'm a kid. And I didn't even tell them I was ten. They just guessed. Even though I typed it up and everything. And made graphs! In color!"

Nora wasn't going to cry in front of her father. She wasn't. If she had to cry, she was going to do it later, alone with her ants.

"Honey," her father said, "I think it's wonderful that you tried to publish your article. How many ten-year-olds would even try?"

"An eleven-year-old girl tried and succeeded," Nora shot back. "Her name was Emily Rosa. She's in the *Guinness World Records* book."

"An eleven-year-old published an article in *Nature?*" her father asked, sounding incredulous.

"No, not in *Nature,* but it was in some grown-up science journal."

"Well, sweetie, some journals are easier to publish in than others. *Nature* is one of the very hardest. It might be too much to expect to publish in the *very* top journals right away. And even though you've been learning so much about ants, you only spent a few days on your experiment, right? Some scientists work on their experiments for years. For decades, even."

"So I was silly to try. Is that what you're saying?"

"No. It's never silly to try. Everything that has ever happened in the history of science happened because of someone who tried to learn something new about this amazing, fascinating, incredibly complex world of ours."

Nora knew her father wanted to make her feel better.

But she didn't feel better. She didn't feel better at all.

Upstairs in her room, she didn't want to look at her ants. Even the sight of their busy scurrying and tunneling wasn't going to cheer up a ten-year-old who was too young to be taken seriously by her fellow ant scientists.

How could they not think it was interesting and important that ants wouldn't cross a chalk line unless they had an important reason to cross it? She had probably proven single-handedly that ants could not only react to the world around them by instinct but also actually *think*.

Maybe it was her handwriting on the envelope that had given her away. Her cursive didn't look like her parents' cursive. It looked like the handwriting of someone who had spent two weeks in third grade in a unit on how to write in cursive. Or maybe the title of her article wasn't catchy, but dumb. After all, she had thought it was dumb when Coach Joe had sung "The Ants Go Marching" the day she had brought her ant farm to school, the day the other girls had screamed and run away.

She blinked back the tears she hadn't let herself cry in front of her father.

Maybe her ants *would* make her feel better. Her

ants didn't know or care that she was only ten. They didn't care that her cursive looked like writing by some kid. They didn't care that she—that *they*—had just been ignored by the editor of a famous science journal.

She walked over to her ant farm to see what they were up to. But then her heart sank. Right now, actually, her ants didn't look as if they knew or cared about much of anything.

The ant farm was strangely still.

Two ants were busy in one of the tunnels, but their activity looked aimless, as if they had lost their way, as if they weren't sure what they were supposed to be doing anymore or why they were supposed to be doing it.

She looked more closely.

The rest of the ants were completely motionless.

Sleeping? All of them?

Or dead?

Some ant queens produce as many daughters as there are people in the whole United States. But only a few million are alive at any time. Ants die a LOT.

Nora had had ants die before.

Dying was one of the things ants did.

This time felt different, though.

These were the ants she had tried to show to her unappreciative classmates. These were the ants that had led to an important scientific discovery that might have even proved that ants could think.

Nora didn't just love ants in general.

She loved these ants in particular.

But they were definitely dead, all but two of them.

Nora hadn't known that the deaths of creatures so small could leave so big a hole in her heart.

During the morning huddle on Friday, Coach Joe asked who wanted to share their persuasive speeches. Brody's hand was first to shoot in the air, as usual. But this time, to Nora's great surprise, Mason raised his hand, too. Nora decided to volunteer as well. After all, what was the point of a persuasive speech if you didn't use it to try to persuade somebody?

"Great!" Coach Joe said. "Brody, you're up at bat first."

"I changed mine," Brody explained before he started reading. "I was going to write about the colonists and how they shouldn't have a war, but just try to work things out instead. And I did write about that. But then I added something else. About a different war. A war right here in our own class."

Brody's eyes swept the huddle, as if to make sure that everyone was ready to be persuaded of something very important.

"Okay, Brody," Coach Joe said. "Let's hear it."

Don't Have Any Wars
By Brody Baxter

War is a very bad idea. It is always better not to have a war if possible. Whenever there is a war, one side wins and one side loses. But really both sides lose.

The American colonists were mad at the British because their taxes were too high. They were mad because they had to pay taxes on stamps. Then they got even madder because they had to pay taxes on tea. If there was one thing people loved long ago, it was drinking tea. Plus, they were mad because they didn't get to vote on any of these taxes. They thought it wasn't fair to have taxation without representation.

So they started a war. The war did make America free from the British. But thousands of people died on both sides. The soldiers were miserable during the cold winters. They had to walk in the snow with no shoes. The war cost a lot of money, too.

If King George the Third had just let the colonies be their own country, it would have saved lots of lives and lots of money, and the ending would have been just the same. If the colonists had tried to get along better with the British, sooner or later the British would have gotten tired of having colonies anyway. Nobody has colonies anymore today.

So they shouldn't have had a war.

In our own class, we've been having a war of cat people against dog people. The war is hurting a lot of people's feelings. There is no need to have a war in our class. Dog people can love dogs best, but they can still like cats, too. Cat people can love cats best, but they can still like dogs, too. And if they don't, they can just keep quiet and not say mean things about other people's pets.

If the British and Americans hadn't had a war, they could have all been happy.

If cat lovers and dog lovers in our class stop their war, we can all be happy, too.

Brody looked up from his paper with a huge grin.

"Thanks, Brody," Coach Joe said. "I think a lot of us needed to hear that. So, team, is anybody persuaded?"

The huddle burst into applause.

Nora saw Dunk, blushing brick red, whisper something to Emma.

Emma giggled and whispered something back.

Dunk whispered something else.

Emma giggled again.

"Oh, Dunk!" Nora heard her say.

Apparently, Brody's speech had brought about at least one truce in the dog-cat war.

"Mason," Coach Joe said then. "What do you have for us? What do you want to persuade us of?"

Mason began reading:

A Persuasive Speech Against Persuasive Speeches
By Mason Dixon

In our class at school, we are learning how to write persuasive speeches. We are learning how to persuade other people to think and act the way we want them to. I think that before we learn how to persuade people, we should ask ourselves if that is a good thing to do. I say no.

The first reason we shouldn't try to persuade people is that people have a right to think the way they want to think and to do the things they want to do. As long as it doesn't hurt anybody else. Why should everybody think the same way? It's good that people think lots of different things.

The second reason we shouldn't try to persuade people is that it doesn't work. People just decide to keep believing the first thing they believed, only harder. When someone tries too hard to sell something to you, you get suspicious. It makes you want not to buy that thing even more.

The third reason we shouldn't try to persuade people is that it is irritating. In fact, it is very irritating. If someone doesn't like to do new things, and other people, like that person's parents, keep telling him to try new things, that person is going to get irritated and want the other people to stop. If that person only likes brown socks, and macaroni and cheese, and Fig Newtons, that person isn't going to like being told over and over again to wear other-color socks and eat other foods.

So, in conclusion, people shouldn't try to persuade other people. The end.

"Good one!" Coach Joe said once Mason stopped reading. "I never thought of things that way. Team, what do you think?"

Lots of kids clapped this time, too.

"Yup," Coach Joe said. "I think Mason hit that one right out of the ballpark."

A boy named James read an anti-homework persuasive speech. Nora liked that it quoted statistics, which claimed that there was no relationship between how much homework students did at night and how well they scored on standardized tests. She adored statistics. Then a girl named Hazel read a persuasive speech about some celebrity who wore too much makeup and how she would look better with less makeup. That one was dopey, in Nora's opinion. People either liked makeup or didn't, the same way some people liked dogs and some people liked cats. Amy read her speech, which turned out to be about how people in the U.S. should keep pet cats indoors so that they wouldn't keep killing over 2 billion songbirds each year. Nora remembered that, fortunately, Precious Cupcake was already an indoor cat.

"Nora?" Coach Joe called on her.

She picked up her paper and started to read.

The Importance of Studying Science
By Nora Alpers

Many people I know think science is a boring subject. In fact, some of these people are girls in my class at school. Even when girls think science is interesting, they can feel like they're not supposed to, because the other girls they know talk more about boys, clothes, or cats, instead of about batteries, planets, and ants.

This pattern continues when girls grow up. More than half the people in America are female, but less than a quarter of scientists, engineers, mathematicians, and tech workers are women. Only one-fifth of physics PhDs are given to women. Only fourteen percent of physics professors are women. In a whole century, only fifteen women got a Nobel Prize in science.

These are very sad facts, because it is so important that everybody, including girls, knows about science. We need to know about science so that we can protect our planet. Species are going extinct at a faster rate than any other time in human history, because of things that humans do. People do things that cause climate change and loss of habitat. If people knew more about science, they would know not to do these things. More important, if people knew more about science, they wouldn't *want* to do these things. The more you learn about science, the more interesting and important you think everything in the world is. Even little tiny things that most people don't care about, like ants.

So it is important for everybody to learn about science, but especially for girls, because they are getting left out right now. My family is full of women scientists. My mother is a scientist who is an expert on the rings of Saturn. My sister is a scientist who studies rock formations. I want to be a scientist, too, and learn as much as I can about ants.

Even if you don't want to be a scientist, I hope you learn as much as you can about science. Science may not be "cute," but it is interesting, beautiful, and important for our world. The more we all learn about science, the more we can save our world.

Nora took a deep breath when she was done. What would her classmates think? She knew Amy would like it. But would the rest of them be persuaded?

They were all clapping loudly. But they had applauded every speech so far, even the dumb one about celebrity makeup. She doubted that she had actually persuaded anybody, not the way that Brody had. But then, as Coach Joe was closing the huddle by saying something about seeing if the local newspaper might want to publish any of their speeches, Emma leaned over to her.

"I'm sorry, Nora," Emma said. "I shouldn't have screamed that day when your ants came to school. I was definitely being unscientific. I hope you bring your ants to school again sometime soon. I really do."

Even though Nora knew Emma meant well, this

request, following upon the rejection of her ant article *and* the collapse of her entire ant colony, was too much for her to bear.

"I can't," Nora snapped. "They're dead."

"Dead?" Emma asked, as if she couldn't have heard correctly.

"Yes," Nora said brightly. "All of them." The last two had died yesterday. "But thanks for asking."

Before Emma could make any reply, Nora marched off to her desk, took out her math book, and made herself very busy converting fractions to decimals.

In almost every ant colony, once the queen dies, the whole colony dies, ant by ant by ant. Ant colonies die just as individual ants do. But when they die, it's a lot sadder.

15

At lunch, Nora was surprised to see Dunk approach the table with his tray, a sheepish grin on his face.

"I'm here," he said to Emma.

Tamara was absent that day. Emma motioned to Dunk to take Tamara's empty seat.

Nora took notice. A fourth-grade boy was sitting at a fourth-grade girls' cafeteria table. To her knowledge, that had never happened before at Plainfield Elementary School.

"Dunk," Emma announced to the other girls,

"told me that he's interested in seeing some of Precious Cupcake's cat videos."

Dunk made a strangled sound. Nora could tell that he wanted to say that he wasn't *interested* in watching cat videos, but that he had reluctantly agreed to watch them as part of the truce between cat people and dog people. Nora could also tell that he knew better than to point that out.

"Are you ready?" Emma asked him sweetly.

Dunk grunted.

"Girls, which one should I show him first?"

"'Princess Precious,'" Bethy said.

"'Cupcake Capers'!" Elise answered.

"They're all adorable," Amy said, in case there had been any hard feelings over her anti-bird-eating speech.

"Nora?" Emma asked.

Nora knew Emma was trying to be extra-friendly to make up for the deaths of her ants.

"Do you have any videos from the high tea?" Nora asked, because she couldn't think of anything else. "I mean, from the high tea before she swallowed the ribbon?"

As soon as she said it, she realized it was the wrong thing to have said.

"I'll start with 'Princess Precious,'" Emma declared.

She fiddled with her phone for a minute as Dunk shoveled in some hasty mouthfuls of hamburger casserole.

"All right!" Emma chirped. "Here's the first one!"

Dunk put down his fork. Nobody was supposed to watch videos of Precious Cupcake with divided attention.

Emma and Dunk leaned their heads together so they could look at the cat videos at the same time. The other girls got up from their seats and crowded behind them, even though Nora couldn't begin to count how many times they had seen them all before.

"Ohh!"

"So cute!"

"The cutest!"

That, from the girls.

Dunk hadn't yet said anything.

"Dunk, you're supposed to say *ooh* and *aah*," Emma instructed.

Already red, Dunk grew even redder. But there was no halfway point for admiration of Emma's cat videos.

"Ooh," he muttered sullenly. "Aah."

"Say how cute she is," Emma commanded.

Nora wondered if Dunk would bolt back to his own table, where two boys were having a lively duel with their bread sticks.

He didn't.

"She *is* cute," he said, sounding surprised, and surprisingly sincere.

Emma giggled.

"Now let me find the one where she's licking the cupcake frosting. Oh, here it is!"

Dunk gave another grunt of appreciation.

Emma giggled again.

The weekend was a long, empty one, without any ants in it.

Saturday morning, Nora emptied the contents of the ant farm into the backyard, all the sad remains of the formerly bustling ant colony. She set her ant farm on a dusty shelf in the back of the garage.

"You aren't getting any more ants?" her mother asked as they were getting ready to head over to the last Fighting Bulldogs game of the season.

"No," Nora told her. "I'm through with ants."

"You're through with *ants*?"

Why did Nora always have to repeat everything? Didn't people listen the first time? But she knew her mother had heard her; her mother just didn't believe her.

"You never liked my ants anyway," Nora said. It came out sounding like an accusation.

"That's not true."

"It is true. Admit it."

"Okay, I never liked having *stinging* ants *loose* in my kitchen. That much is true. But I definitely liked your ants when they were safe in their farm."

Nora must have looked skeptical, because her mother went on, "Well, I always liked that *you* liked your ants. Your father and I are both so proud of you for being such a serious scientist, studying your ants, doing experiments with them. How many girls your age are already budding myrmecologists? In fact, your father told me that you—"

Nora cut her off with a glare that said, *Don't even go there.* She couldn't stand to hear her mother trying to be like her father and make it sound wonderful that she had even tried to publish her ant article. She didn't want credit for *trying*. She wanted credit for *succeeding*.

"Anyway, we're proud of you," her mother finished.

The Bulldogs won their game. Nora scored the winning basket.

Mason, Brody, and the rest of their teammates were all screaming with excitement when the buzzer sounded.

"Nora! Nora! Nora!" they cheered.

It was amazing how worked up people could get about things that didn't really matter.

After the game, Nora went home to a house with no ants for her to check on. She didn't have any homework to do. Coach Joe had said that in honor of the anti-homework persuasive speech, he'd give them one weekend with no homework at all.

Nora didn't feel like calling Mason and Brody. They were probably busy teaching Dog new tricks or giving him another bath to try to get rid of the last, lingering skunk odor.

She didn't feel like calling any of the girls, even

Amy. They were probably busy talking about how funny Dunk had looked watching Emma's cat videos and how the cat videos really were the cutest videos in the history of the world. Amy would be busy with her whole household full of still-living pets.

She didn't feel like disturbing her parents. They were both hunched over the computers in their home offices, probably busy writing articles to be published in prestigious grown-up science journals.

She didn't feel like doing anything.

Monday morning, Nora found a pale blue envelope on her desk. Her name was written on it in round printing that could only have been done by a girl. The *o* in *Nora* had petals around it to form a flower.

The envelope contained a card with a picture of a rainbow on the front of it, with fancy script that read:

With Deepest Sympathy on the Loss of Your Pets

Someone had added an *s* to *Pet* to make it read *Pets*.

Inside the card was a printed poem:

Pets are angels in disguise.
They give us joy and love.
When they finally pass away,
They watch us from above.

From Heaven your pets are looking down
And sent me here to say
The love they give is never lost
But still with you today.

The card was signed: Emma.

Nora didn't know whether to cry or laugh.

As much as she missed her ants, she couldn't think of them as angels, even as *very* well-disguised angels.

She didn't think they were in heaven watching her and hoping Emma would give her a card about them.

She had loved her ants. But she couldn't honestly say that they had loved her back.

That wasn't what ants *did*.

"Huddle time!" Coach Joe called out. "Hurry on over, team. I have some good news to share."

Nora found a place next to Mason and Brody.

"My parents read my anti-persuasive persuasive speech," Mason told her.

"And?"

"They weren't persuaded."

Nora laughed.

"Actually, they were sort of persuaded. My mom said I still have to try new foods sometimes. And go new places. But I don't have to do figure skating! And I don't have to take voice lessons. My dad looked pretty thrilled about it. I don't think he wanted to have to listen to me practice."

Nora laughed again.

"All right, team," Coach Joe said. "Here's today's paper, hot off the press: the *Plainfield Daily Record.*"

Nora's parents got the *Plainfield Daily Record,* but they hadn't had time to read it this morning.

"Well, on the op-ed page today—that's the page *opposite* the *editorial* page—there is a piece by one of our classmates. A persuasive speech about the importance of getting more kids, especially girls, to study science. Congratulations, Nora!"

Nora was bewildered. But then she remembered that Coach Joe had said something about seeing if the newspaper might want to publish their speeches. Apparently, they had. And the one they wanted to publish was hers.

This time, the applause from her classmates was more than polite. It sounded more like the cheers of the Fighting Bulldogs after she had scored the winning basket.

Her persuasive speech wasn't published in *Nature*. It wasn't going to set any Guinness World Record for youngest article by anyone ever. But right now it felt pretty sweet to have Coach Joe hold up the newspaper, folded open to the page where her article appeared, framed in a little box:

THE IMPORTANCE OF STUDYING SCIENCE
By Nora Alpers

Nora is a fourth-grade student
at Plainfield Elementary School.

Part of her wished they hadn't printed her grade. Maybe they had published her article because it was good for a fourth grader, not because it was good, period.

Then again, she *was* a fourth grader. And the newspaper editors obviously thought it was impressive that a fourth grader had written an article good enough to be published.

When the applause had died down, Coach Joe said, "So, Nora, speaking of getting kids more interested in science, what do you think? Will you give us another chance with your ant farm?"

Nora heard Emma's gasp.

"Coach Joe," Emma blurted out, "Nora can't bring her ant farm in again. Because, you see, her ants are—well, they're . . ." She lowered her voice to avoid saying the final word too loudly. "They're *deceased.*"

Coach Joe turned to Nora, as if to confirm the truth of this terrible statement.

Nora thought for a moment before speaking.

"My ants did die. My colony didn't have a queen, and without a queen, a colony dies out in a few weeks or months. That's the life span of the worker ants. But it's okay when ants die. It's part of the life cycle. Ants go through four different stages in their lives: egg, larva, pupa, adult. Once they're adults, they do their work to help the colony survive. Then they die. It's what ants *do*."

She looked around at her classmates, all of them seeming to be listening hard to every word she spoke, even Dunk. Maybe next, Dunk would be agreeing to watch ant videos.

"I'm going to get more ants soon," Nora told the class.

Had she really just said that? Apparently, she had.

"It's winter now, so I don't think I can find any outside in nature. Maybe next summer, I can find more ants in my backyard and even find a queen to go with them. But for now, I can send away on-line to get more ants shipped to me in the mail. I'll bring them in once I get them."

She hadn't spoken the truth to her mother, even though she had thought what she said was true at the time.

She wasn't through with ants.

She was never going to be through with ants.

She'd always want to study ants and learn about them. Maybe she *would* publish an article in

Nature someday, when she had studied ants for years and years.

She was going to study ants forever.

After all, studying ants was what Nora *did*.

Fascinating ant fact:

There are only 500 myrmecologists in the world.

Counting me, 501!

ACKNOWLEDGMENTS

It is a joy to be able to thank some of the wonderful people who helped bring this book into being. It was during breakfast with my brilliant editor, Nancy Hinkel, that I paid attention when she said, "I could use a book about a girl with an ant farm!" Her encouragement and enthusiasm fueled Nora's love of ants on every page. I received careful critique on early drafts from my longtime Boulder writing group (Marie DesJardin, Mary Peace Finley, Ann Whitehead Nagda, Leslie O'Kane, Phyllis Perry, and Elizabeth Wrenn). Professor Whitney Cranshaw of Colorado State University gave generously of his time and expertise to talk with me about ants (any ant-related errors in the book are, of course, my own). I looked at Katie Kath's adorable first sketches for the book and said, "There she is! There's Nora!"

Thanks also to my wise and caring agent, Stephen Fraser; consistently helpful Stephen Brown; magnificently sharp-eyed copy editors Esther Lin, Steph Engel, and Artie Bennett; and Isabel Warren-Lynch and Trish Parcell for their appealing book design.

Most of Nora's fascinating ant facts are drawn from *Journey to the Ants: A Story of Scientific Exploration* by Bert Hölldobler and Edward O. Wilson, Cambridge, Mass.: Belknap Press, 1994. On behalf of Nora and all budding myrmecologists everywhere, I am grateful to them for this amazing book.

Claudia Mills is the author of over fifty books for young readers, including the Mason Dixon series. She does not personally keep an ant farm, but she does have a cat, Snickers, with whom she curls up on her couch at home in Boulder, Colorado, drinking hot chocolate and writing. Visit her at claudiamillsauthor.com.

improv
wisdom

improv
wisdom

don't
prepare,
just
show up

PATRICIA RYAN MADSON

Bell Tower · New York

Grateful acknowledgment is made to Coleman Barks for permission to
reprint an excerpt from "Two Kinds of Intelligence," from *The Essential Rumi*
by Rumi, translated by Coleman Barks. Copyright © 1995 by Coleman
Barks. Reprinted by permission of the translator.

Grateful acknowledgment to reprint "All The Good" by Jana Stanfield,
copyright © 2003 Jana Stan Tunes (ASCAP). From the Jana Stanfield
Album: *LET THE CHANGE BEGIN*. www.JanaStanfield.com.
Phone Number(s): 615.333.7550 or 888.530.5262

All rights reserved. Published in the United States by Bell Tower,
an imprint of the Crown Publishing Group, a division of
Random House, Inc., New York.
www.crownpublishing.com

BELL TOWER and colophon are registered trademarks
of Random House, Inc.

Library of Congress Cataloging-in-Publication Data
Madson, Patricia Ryan.
Improv wisdom: don't prepare, just show up /
Patricia Ryan Madson. — 1st ed. Includes bibliographical
references. I. Conduct of life.   I. Title.
BF637.C5M325   2005
158 — dc22   2004026352
ISBN 1-4000-8188-2

Printed in the United States of America

DESIGN BY LAUREN DONG

18   20   19

For Mama,
Virginia Louise Pittman Ryan
1920–1998
She always said yes.

———

For my husband,
Ronald Whitney Madson
My improv partner in life

It delights me to acknowledge my deep gratitude
to the four decades of students who have shown up for my classes,
and
who tried all the crazy things I recommended.
It is thanks to each of you that I have had
the greatest job in the world—
being a teacher.

[contents]

There are two kinds of intelligence: one acquired,
as a child in school memorizes facts and concepts
from books and from what the teacher says,
collecting information from the traditional sciences
as well as from the new sciences.

With such intelligence you rise in the world.
You get ranked ahead or behind others
in regard to your competence in retaining
information. You stroll with this intelligence
in and out of fields of knowledge, getting always more
marks on your preserving tablets.

There is another kind of tablet, one
already completed and preserved inside you.
A spring overflowing its springbox. A freshness
in the center of the chest. This other intelligence
does not turn yellow or stagnate. It's fluid,
and it doesn't move from outside to inside
through the conduits of plumbing-learning.

This second knowing is a fountainhead
from within you, moving out.

—RUMI, "TWO KINDS OF INTELLIGENCE,"
translated by Coleman Barks

[prologue]

When I was eleven years old and living in Richmond, Virginia, my mother bought me a paint-by-numbers kit. The subject was a leafy maple tree. I loved the silky feel of the brushes, the touch of the textured canvas, and the oily smell of the paints. I painted carefully, always getting the prescribed colors just right, critical if I went over a line even slightly. My formula painting seemed beautiful to me, and my father declared proudly: "Patsy is an artist." Other kits followed, and I faithfully continued to paint inside the lines.

I had found the way to live: Always go by the rules. Use the recipe. Follow the pattern. Rehearse the script. Copy the masters. I followed the lines in everything I did, even though I considered myself an artist, a theater artist at first. With theater, you were given your lines, and all you had to do was bring them to life. That seemed easy. I went to study at Wayne State University to get a graduate degree so that I could teach. After three years with the Hilberry Classic Repertory Company and several hundred performances, I moved on to accept an assistant professorship at Denison University in Ohio, teaching acting. I longed to be normal and have a dependable and ordinary life. I rented a house perched on a hill in Granville, Ohio, began collecting furniture and art, and cultivated a coterie of university friends and colleagues.

This was the job of my dreams. I had a regular (albeit modest) paycheck, generous benefits, the prestige of being a professor, long holidays, and the security of being part of a small college family. My one goal in life was to make that dream permanent—and the way to do that was to gain tenure. I studied the politics of the university and volunteered for any task that would look good on my academic résumé. I chaired the Governance Review Commission. I took on a prestigious assignment as Denison's regional director for the Great Lakes Colleges Association New York Arts Program. I allied myself with the right people. I taught nine different classes in my department, volunteering to fill any void that appeared in the curriculum. I was popular and, in my fifth year, won a university prize for excellence in teaching. My résumé of college service, professional activity, and classroom experience seemed flawless. The tenure review came, and my interviews went well. I was all set to put a down payment on a home in Granville when the decision was announced.

Sorry.

The notification letter thanked me for my considerable service and informed me that my teaching "lacked intellectual distinction." This made no sense to me, since I had recently won a teaching award, had chosen each career move to impress the academy, and had done everything by the book. I had painted inside the lines—well. So where had I gone wrong?

I had never taken a chance. I had not once followed an impulse or listened to the beat of my own drum. Polonius's instruction "To thine own self be true" flashed in mind. I had not been true to my self. It had not occurred to me that there was another way of living that did not require a script. To find that way I would need to learn to listen to and trust myself. (The *real* discovery came years later when I understood that I had to trust something greater than myself.)

I had tried to be worthy of receiving tenure. I didn't understand that this worthiness could come only from honoring my own voice. Making decisions solely to please others is a formula destined to fail. The people I admired were not looking over their shoulders to see if their peers were applauding. They were heeding their inner promptings. "I do this because I know it needs to be done." My search for validation had diverted me from discerning what was uniquely mine.

Denison was right to let me go. Once I had been denied tenure I imagined my academic career to be finished and that it would be unlikely for me to find another university job. I was wrong, fortunately. Before I had even served out a lame-duck year, the chairman of Penn State University's lively theater program offered me an assistant professorship, teaching acting and voice. Someone had left a position on short notice, and I was a qualified candidate. I was overjoyed to have been given another chance.

I promised myself that whatever happened I would never again make choices simply to impress others or to gain status. I would listen to my own drum and march to it. And while I was commonly clumsy with the sticks, I began drumming, so to speak. I gave up doing things "for my résumé." I took up tai chi and spent summers dancing and traveling, studying Eastern religion and expanding my vision of life. My view of theater was no longer bounded by the proscenium arch. I was drawn to the anthropology of acting, and I began to explore, dream, and act. I opened my eyes, looked around, and said yes. I didn't know it at the time, but I was becoming an improviser, learning to listen and to trust my imagination.

Two years later Stanford University enticed me away from Penn State by offering me the job of heading up their undergraduate acting program. It seems no accident that my academic life began to flower at the same time I was exploring this valuable life lesson of improvisation. California was where I needed to be, and in the summer of 1977, in a rusty mint green Mercury Marquis Brougham with shiny brocade seats, I drove across the United States to accept my exciting position on the "Farm."

Painting Outside the Lines

During a trip to Kyoto in the early 1980s, I found myself searching for picture postcards to send home. Instead of selling cards singly, the Japanese prefer to offer a selection of cards in small packs. As I wandered the street looking for single cards, I stumbled into an art-supply store, where I pulled out my dictionary and carefully asked for "hagaki, onegaishimasu" ("postcards, please"). The smiling salesgirl rushed over to a case and pulled out a block of twelve postcards. However, they were blank and made of watercolor paper. She put them on the counter, pleased that she had understood my request. And before I had time to explain that I was actually looking for scenic views, she had placed alongside the tablet a tiny watercolor paint set, half the size of the cards. It contained a miniature brush that could be extended by using the cap to elongate the tip. Charmed by this offer, and not wishing to disappoint the helpful clerk, I purchased the paints and cards and left the store.

I walked to a park near a temple and sat on a bench, looking at peach-colored azaleas in a carefully tended garden. I had a small plastic container, part of some packaging of cookies, and I filled it with water from a drinking fountain. I opened the watercolor set, took out the blank cards and sat wondering what would happen. I remembered

Dad's pronouncement: "Patsy is an artist." I laughed at the thought. I'm not, of course, and since I'm not, it doesn't matter what I do. Why not just play with the paints and see what happens? And so I began to improvise. I looked at the azalea and dabbed my brush in the little paint box. A whoosh of peach, a splash of green . . . a flower, a tree. The lines and numbers had all disappeared. Now I could discover what was there.

Life is an improvisation, and if we are lucky, a long one. It may end unexpectedly, and for some, too soon. I won't be the first author to remind readers to seize the day, to live each precious moment fully and with gusto. Students who believed that something was missing in their lives were drawn to my classes because they thought improv might have an answer (even while doubting their ability to do it). They imagined improvisers as part of some inner circle of talent, endowed with magical abilities or special wit and charm.

I know that improvisation has nothing to do with wit, glibness, or comic ability. A good improviser is someone who is awake, not entirely self-focused, and moved by a desire to do something useful and give something back and who acts upon this impulse. My students wanted to know the password for joining the society of such people, to play fearlessly, and to work with greater ease.

Here is the password—it is *yes!* Understanding the power of yes is easy; practicing that acceptance and affirmation in daily life becomes our challenge.

I'm writing to encourage you to improvise your life, please. I want you to take chances and do more of the things that are important to you. I'm hoping that you will make more mistakes, laugh more often, and have some adventures. I'd be very pleased if you began observing the details of our human interdependence; in particular, seeing those who are contributing to your welfare, right now, and who probably go unnoticed. And I would clap my hands with delight if I learned that you had done something new and worthwhile after using the advice in this book.

What is heartening to me is the growing pile of mash notes, testimonials, and e-mails from former students, undergraduate and adult, who have tried improv and found encouragement and answers. Their stories, which are true, illustrate the journey of opening oneself to possibility. I have created new names for many of the characters here, out of respect for their confidences. I hope some of my students will recognize themselves in these pages.

We have all become more cautious, less inclined to risk anything in our post–9/11 world. Safety has become the greatest good. Homeland security is the nation's watchword. We are staying inside and watching more television. Travel, one of life's great forms of improvisation, has fallen off dramatically. And if national security isn't what is bothering us, it is easy to avoid doing anything new for fear of personal failure or looking silly. We are rapidly becoming a nation of naysayers and stay-at-homes. The double-edged sword of technology has given us tools that eliminate even the need for leaving the house to check out a video. There is almost nothing we can't buy at home, sitting comfortably in our pajamas at a computer terminal. And when we do go out, is it mainly to shop, to go to the mall? Is it just too much trouble to be a good neighbor or friend? What is happening to our daily life and to our dreams?

What is missing in your life? The paperweight on my

desk challenges me to ask the bumper-sticker question: "What would you do if you knew you would not fail?" What would *you* do?

As improvisers we discover that we don't need this unrealistic guarantee to begin. The only real failure is not doing anything. Why not explore, get moving on your life, kickstart your dreams, paint outside the lines? This book will provide inspiration and practical suggestions. Try them.

The Improvisers' World

There's a secret society, known to the initiated as "the improv world." I've been a member of this circle since the 1980s and even founded the Stanford Improvisors, who are part of an international web of groups with such colorful names as Legally Dead Parrots, Bay Area Theatresports™, True Fiction Magazine, Without a Net, and The Purple Crayon. This loosely knit network is focused around the study and performance of improvised theater. They are "'Yes' sayers."

It is easy to be around these folks. They are can-do people. They have learned a way of working together on stage that commonly spills over into their daily lives. There is a spirit of cooperation. If I forget something, my colleagues cover for me. Everyone seems to say "thank you" often, and "I'm sorry" slips naturally off the tongue. We smile and laugh a lot. We rarely need committee meetings to decide things. We do stuff. We make mistakes, sometimes whoppers. We correct them or we capitalize on them. We notice how much others are doing for us. We have fun. We screw up; we apologize. We get on one another's nerves sometimes. We move on. We create life and art together.

We improvise. Keith Johnstone's encouraging quotation from *Impro* reminds us that this habit can be acquired:

> There are people who prefer to say "Yes," and there
> are people who prefer to say "No." Those who say
> "Yes" are rewarded by the adventures they have, and
> those who say "No" are rewarded by the safety they
> attain. There are far more "No" sayers around than
> "Yes" sayers, but you can train one type to behave like
> the other.

"I could never do that," says an observer watching players invent a story together on stage. But you can. These people aren't special in the sense of having uncommon talents. There are no Robin Williams–type comic geniuses among us. We are ordinary folk just like you. The truth is, human beings are improvisers by nature.

Today there are more than 293 million Americans who will need to improvise. Everybody, unless performing a scripted play, makes up his life as he goes along. We are all improvising. Why not do it like a professional? Improvisation is a metaphor, a path, and a system; it is a modus operandi that anyone can learn. Imagine a life brimming with spontaneity. See yourself coping effortlessly with a demanding boss, a tired child, an unexpected turn of fate. Hear yourself speaking at a meeting without a script. Feel yourself alive, poised, and ready for any adventure. Learn simple techniques used for centuries by actors and musicians, and discover how to apply them to your life. The world of improv is a portal into mindfulness and magic.

I learned these principles while teaching the art and wizardry of improvisation over three decades as a drama professor at Stanford, working as a creativity consultant to corporations, and serving as a private counselor. Apart from jazz, until the last decade the medium for learning improvisation has been theater training. During the rise of the dot-coms, improvisation training became popular with entrepreneurs, engineers, people in job transition, stay-at-home moms, and Zen and yoga students, as well as theater folks. Recently it has come into its own as a paradigm that can be used for corporate training, team building, psychological interventions, education, and personal growth. Couples, families, work units, clubs, and neighborhoods can also grow using improvisation. But what about in our daily life, where we have no choice but to improvise? The maxims of improv can help us meet real-life challenges more skillfully, and with a sense of humor.

"Improv is a kind of tai chi for the soul," wrote a former student in my Continuing Studies class; it provides a workout that helps to shake loose rigid patterns of thinking and doing. For many of us, age produces an increased tendency to rely on known patterns, if not an all-out petrifaction. It becomes harder to take risks. We rely on conservative choices and hold on to what we know or perceive to be security. It becomes more natural to say no. Criticism and complaints come more easily. The vibrancy of our life seems to be dimming. Keith Johnstone speaks of this as the world becoming "grayer."

As this dulling of perception bleeds (or expands) onto the canvas of our daily life, a longing may emerge to reconnect with our own creative force, to see the world in color again. This accounts, no doubt, for the popularity of Julia Cameron's *The Artist's Way,* a how-to book for those who want to recapture the artist within. Like Cameron, I believe we are all artists. We just need to show up and begin the activity.

Clearly, there are many paths that can lead toward the opening of the creative self. The practice of improvisation (in contrast, say, to that of writing or painting) teaches something that we are hungry to understand: how to be in harmony with one another and how to have fun. We practice improvisation not only to "express ourselves" but to connect with others in a more immediate way.

Improvising invites us to lighten up and look around. It offers an alternative to the controlling way many of us try to lead our lives. It requires that we say yes and be helpful rather than argumentative; it offers us a chance to do things differently. These ideas will seem familiar to those who have studied Eastern thought.

My training and inspiration come from two sources: one from the drama theories of Keith Johnstone, author of the classic text on improvisation, *Impro,* and founder of International Theatresports,™ and the other from the world of psychology. Dr. David K. Reynolds, anthropologist and international authority on Japanese psychology, developed a paradigm known as Constructive Living®. Ideas from this life way are embedded in the maxims of improv. The teachings of Johnstone and Reynolds have been deep rivers for me. Nearly ten years ago I felt them flow together in my work in the classroom. The improv stage became the platform and laboratory where the psychology of purposeful living could be taught and practiced indirectly. Students showed up for fun but left with useful advice.

My debt to these creative men is immeasurable. My personal life has been enriched and stabilized by applying the knowledge from their two worlds. It is their combined wisdom that pervades this book. I would like to invite everyone to become an improviser. Join our elite club right now. Remember that you already have the password, which is *yes*!

The First Improvisers

Long before there was planning, there was improvising. For millennia humans functioned naturally *only* by thinking on their feet, problem-solving in the here and now. I wake up. I look around carefully. I hunt for food. I share it with my fellow primates. We find a warm, dry place to sleep. We have a few laughs.

At some point, however, survival demanded planning; the cave folk who wolfed down just the berries at hand and trout only as it swam by didn't make it through the long, freezing winters. To stay alive, early man needed to cultivate the capacity to think ahead and stow away food for the lean times. This development in human history marked the end of improvising as our primary modus vivendi. Enter the appointment calendar. We learned to worry about the future. This growth into higher brain functioning came with a long-term cost.

Leapfrogging thousands of years into the present, we find ourselves nearly strangled by the planning instinct. For some of us it *is* our life. We plan when we should execute. We make lists, worry, or theorize (often endlessly) when we ought to be responding. We choose safety above all else. We seem to have lost the knack of looking at the day with fresh eyes or doing anything out of our comfort zone.

While an ordinary day may be punctuated by the rituals of getting out of bed, filling the coffeemaker, taking in the paper, going to work, and sitting down at our desk or workstation, what actually goes on (both the specific content and the quality of these behaviors) is always changing. Reality continually presents itself as a fresh moment. I have the choice of going through the motions, plodding along half asleep, or waking up to my life. I can choose to do things differently right now.

Is improvisation a skill that can be learned? You bet. You may be surprised to learn that it is actually a *method* of working. There are rules of conduct about what to do and how to pay attention while you are creating in the spur of the moment. (For example, an improviser learns to memorize a name the first time it is mentioned.)

Improvising can give us a taste of the primal freedom that our early ancestors experienced before they turned their attention to planning; it is an exhilarating way to live. Charles Darwin recognized the value of this when he wrote, "In the long history of humankind (and animalkind, too) those who learned to collaborate and improvise most effectively have prevailed." While our body knowledge of the art of improv seems to be cellular, most of us don't consider ourselves to be improvisers. We all fear the unknown and doubt our ability to respond spontaneously, even though we have seen countless examples of this talent at work. The adrenaline that fills us when we are helping someone in an emergency is a reminder that we are improvisers by nature.

Then there is the stumbling block of humor.

Not Everything Is Funny

There is a common misunderstanding that improvisation is primarily the study of comedy. Some improv does yield comedy. The popularity of Drew Carey's *Whose Line Is It Anyway?*

has been a mixed blessing for the improv world. Television viewers now equate improv with the fast-paced utterances of Wayne Brady and his witty cohorts. Yes, these funny actors are creating comedic sketches on the spot. However, improv as a method is used for much more than comedy. It is also a time-honored way to explore dramatic situations or the nature of a character in the theater, as well as to create music and dance.

On the home front, some improvisations produce a delicious dinner, a last-minute handmade birthday card, or words of appreciation at a retirement party. Fixing a flat tire is usually an improvisation. All of parenting is improvised; no book prepares us for it. All conversation—indeed, all natural speech, if you think about it—is an improvisation. Unless you are performing a memorized text or a rehearsed speech, whenever you speak you are improvising.

Understanding how the improv system works can lead you to act more like a skilled jazz musician and less like a tuba player who has dropped her sheet music. Winging it need not be terrifying. This book will introduce you to the laws of improv—improv maxims, I call them. Each chapter will explain how a particular principle works, point out common obstacles, and offer some "try this" exercises. When you come across an exercise that appeals to you, put it into practice right away, if possible. I've included a variety of them, hoping that everyone who reads this book will experiment with a few.

An excellent manual on swimming is useless until you jump into the pool. Getting wet is what it's all about. So it is with improvising. My aim is to nudge you out of your comfortable poolside chair, guide you as you climb onto the high board, and cheer you on as you dive into the clear, crystal water. Or perhaps you find yourself slogging through some murky marsh instead of looking at a cool swimming pool. Improv may help you there as well.

When Not to Improvise

Keep in mind that improvisation is a tool and should always be put into service with a healthy dose of common sense. It is a way of doing things that emphasizes a flexible mind and a sense of humor; it is not a scientific method. While there is much in life that requires thoughtful planning, even the most meticulously scripted event (a wedding, for example) will have moments that come alive when improvised. The most believable performances in the traditional theater have the quality of an improvisation; they seem to be happening in real time. We value the authentic, the spontaneous.

A successful life involves both planning and improvising. Sometimes we actually do need a script. Those scripts that are working well for us (positive habits, for example) should be preserved and treasured. Spontaneity for its own sake is never the key. Knowing which strategy to use involves examining things clearly. Our moment-to-moment experience is improvisational, even though it exists within a structure or plan. That is, life brings us opportunities, questions, and problems to solve, and we respond in real time, trying to make sense out of each challenge or offer. *How* we live our lives within the structure of our day is an eternal improvisation.

The invitation to improvise is not a prescription for a careless approach to life. True improvisation is always an act of responsibility; it implies a conscious morality. We may know individuals who flaunt spontaneity as the supreme virtue and excuse thoughtless or selfish behavior in the name of "going with the flow." I am reminded of an inscription on a gold-lettered plaque over the oak bar in a Welsh pub: PISCES MORTUI SOLUM CUM FLUMINE NATANT. ("Only dead fish go with the flow.") Failure to plan can have real consequences. Scheduling medical checkups is important. It is a good idea to buy airline tickets in advance, fill up the gas tank before the fuel gauge signals empty, and pay a parking ticket the day you receive it. Retirement savings is best started decades in advance.

You are always the one steering the canoe, however. Sometimes on the white-water-rapids course it is both relaxing and exhilarating to be swept along by the swells, oars at rest, watching the scenery and marveling at the ease of it all. And sometimes we must paddle like hell against the current in order to take a fork in the river.

In 1982 I took a year off from teaching to circumnavigate the globe. I bought a one-way, around-the-world airline ticket. I was allowed to make as many stops as I liked, in the line of direction, but couldn't backtrack or go too far north or south of my last stop, and I had to complete my journey within twelve months. Buying the ticket gave me a sense of stability (planning); experiencing all the places was the great adventure. Planning provided a platform for me to improvise. Taking an improvised step always leads you somewhere.

Notice where you are going.

[the first maxim]
say yes

. . . yes I said yes I will Yes.

—JAMES JOYCE, *Ulysses*

this is going to sound crazy. Say yes to everything.
Accept all offers. Go along with the plan. Support someone else's dream. Say "yes"; "right"; "sure"; "I will"; "okay";
"of course"; "YES!" Cultivate all the ways you can imagine to
express affirmation. When the answer to all questions is yes,
you enter a new world, a world of action, possibility, and adventure. Molly Bloom's famous line from *Ulysses* draws us
into her ecstasy. Humans long to connect. Yes glues us together. Yes starts the juices rolling. Yes gets us into heaven
and also into trouble. Trouble is not so bad when we are in it
together, actually.

The world of yes may be the single most powerful secret
of improvising. It allows players who have no history with
one another to create a scene effortlessly, telepathically.
Safety lies in knowing your partner will go along with whatever idea you present. Life is too short to argue over which
movie to see. Seize the first idea and go with it. Don't con-
fuse this with being a "yes-man," implying mindless pander-
ing. Saying yes is an act of courage and optimism; it allows
you to share control. It is a way to make your partner happy.
Yes expands your world.

Gertrude, one of my adult students and a mother of three small children, reported a lively adventure based on her application of this maxim. "Friday, my eight-year-old, Samantha, burst into the kitchen with a gleam in her eyes. 'Mommy, Mommy, there's a monster in the closet!' she shrieked. Normally, I would have thought my best reply to be a reality check for her. I would have said something like: 'No, dear, there is no monster in the closet. It's just your imagination, sweetie.' Instead, considering the rule of yes, I turned from the dishes I was washing and said: 'There is? Wow, let's go see!' I accompanied her to the closet, where we had a dynamic encounter with the monster, capturing it and squealing with delight as we tickled it into disappearing. It was a magical shared adventure. I would never have thought of joining Samantha's fantasy before considering the rule of yes! Thanks, improv."

It is undoubtedly an exaggeration to suggest that we can say yes to everything that comes up, but we can all say yes to more than we normally do. Once you become aware that you can, you will see how often we use the technique of blocking in personal relationships simply out of habit. Turning this around can bring positive and unexpected results.

I can remember the day nearly forty years ago when I made a conscious decision to adopt the yes rule. I was attending a tai chi workshop, and a woman whom I hardly knew asked if I could give her a ride home. I normally shy away from encounters with strangers, much preferring silence over casual social exchange. My heart sinks if I find myself with a chatty airplane seat-mate who wants to talk for the entire flight. I couldn't find a good reason to say no, so I said yes. She climbed into my car, and I pulled the old Chevy onto the freeway. As we searched politely for areas of common interest, the conversation turned to our tai chi experience and our physical well-being. I learned that she, too, had some problems with lower back pain. We commiserated, and she offered the name of a wise and skillful acupuncturist who had helped her considerably. As we parted, she wrote down the name and phone number of the healer and handed it to me while thanking me for the ride. What struck me at that moment was my wrongheadedness. I had thought that I was doing her a favor in giving her a ride, when it seemed (and here we get into some metaphysical difficulty with language) reality (the universe? my guardian angel?) was actually offering me some help. The acupuncturist turned out to be a godsend. I would not have found him without the connection with the woman I drove home. "Always say yes if someone asks for help and you can give it," I vowed. I admit a selfish motive in adopting this rule at that time, but the maxim has become a great teacher. Who benefits as we say yes to life? Notice.

Saying yes (and following through with support) prevents you from committing a cardinal sin—blocking. Blocking comes in many forms; it is a way of trying to control the situation instead of accepting it. We block when we say no, when we have a better idea, when we change the subject, when we correct the speaker, when we fail to listen, or when we simply ignore the situation. The critic in us wakes up and runs the show. Saying no is the most common way we attempt to control the future. For many of us the habit is so ingrained that we don't notice we are doing it. We are not only experienced at blocking others, we commonly block ourselves. "I'm not good at brush painting, so why bother? Whatever made me think I could do art?" "I'll never be the

cook that Mom was, so I might as well order take-out."
Blocking is often cleverly disguised as the critical or academic perspective. Finding fault is its hallmark. A sophisti-
cated critic may even appear to be agreeing by offering the
"yes *but*" response. Try substituting "yes *and*" for "yes but"—
this will get the ball rolling.

The spirit of improvising is embodied in the notion of
"yes and." Agreement begins the process; what comes next is
to add something or develop the offer in a positive direction. Avoiding this next step is a form of blocking. I once
taught a student who was scared to add anything to a scene
unless he was instructed to do so. I think he was afraid of
making a mistake. If Martha walked over to him on stage
and proffered an imaginary ice-cream cone, Sheldon would
accept the cone and just stand there, holding it. He appeared positive, seemed to be saying yes to the offer. But
nothing else happened. Sheldon just stood there, blankly,
until Martha advanced the scene by saying: "The elephants
are coming right after these clowns." Sheldon's unwillingness to add something to the story became a kind of aggres-
sion. Players learn that sharing the control of the story is the
only way to really have a good time. The rule of "yes and"
can be used in relationships. Build upon someone else's
dream. And when you are meeting new people, it is helpful
to volunteer information about yourself, your interests,
hobbies, dreams. This can open a door to friendship.

try this:

Support someone else's dreams. Pick a person
(your spouse, child, boss), and, for a week, agree with

all of her ideas. Find something right about everything he says or does. Look for every opportunity to offer support. Consider her convenience and time preferences ahead of your own. Give him the spotlight. Notice the results.

As we practice this affirmative response to life, positive things can happen. Kathleen Norris, in *Amazing Grace,* points out the connection between the impulse to say yes and our capacity for faith. "An alert human infant, at about one month of age, begins to build a vocabulary, making sense of the chaos of sound that bombards the senses. . . . Eventually the rudiments of words come; often 'Mama,' 'Dada,' 'Me,' and the all-purpose 'No!' An unqualified 'Yes' is a harder sell, to both children and adults. To say 'yes' is to make a leap of faith, to risk oneself in a new and often scary relationship. Not being quite sure of what we are doing or where it will lead us, we try on assent, we commit ourselves to affirmation. With luck, we find our efforts are rewarded. The vocabulary of faith begins."

I can't remember a time in history when the need for optimism and affirmation has been greater. In an article that examined how prevailing film sensibilities portrayed the question of individuality on screen in the last century, *San Francisco Chronicle* critic Mick LaSalle made this shocking claim: "American movies [2004] are more cynical and despairing than before. Their implicit message: people are garbage and the world is terrifying."[1] Negative images surround us. Unimaginable horrors are now part of our collective unconscious.

With the rule of yes, we call upon our capacity to envision, to create new and positive images. This yes invites us to find out what is right about the situation, what is good about the offer, what is worthy in the proposal. Exercising the yes muscle builds optimism. However, we sensibly understand that the practice of affirmation is not a guarantee of outcomes. Saying yes to life will not banish problems or promise eternal success. A positive perspective is a constructive one, however, and it is easier on those around us.

try this:

For one day say yes to everything. Set your own preferences aside. Notice the results. See how often it may not be convenient or easy to do this.

Obviously, use common sense in executing this rule. If you are a diabetic and are offered a big piece of pie, you'll need to find a way to protect your health. Perhaps you can say boldly, "Yes, I'd love to have this pie to take home to my son who adores cherries."

Inventing Proverbs

There is wisdom in all of us. A beloved game that I learned from Rebecca Stockley, a professional improviser and educator, involves inventing a new proverb by speaking it one word at a time. This is done by a group of players who add the next most logical word to what has gone before. Do this quickly without "thinking" of a good idea. When it is clear that the proverb is finished (and this seems to happen by a natural consensus), all the players put on a "knowing, wise look," tap their fingers together in a prayerlike mudra, and say, "Yes, yes, yes, yes, yes . . . ," affirming the wisdom of whatever sage or nonsense aphorism has been invented by the group. It is very easy to teach and to play this game, and it often releases a lot of laughter.

Liz, a graduate student in product design, stayed after class one day to share a story. She had just returned from being at home with her family, who were all reeling from the sad news of a cancer diagnosis for their father. "Everyone has been so disheartened about this that I thought we needed a little cheering," said Liz. "Improv was our tonic. I taught the Proverbs game to the family, and we sat around the dinner table playing it. We were all actually able to laugh at the sometimes wise and often crazy sayings that we created together. We needed this laughter."

"Always . . . look . . . before . . . crossing . . . a . . . chicken." Yes, yes, yes, yes, yes!

"Try . . . not . . . to . . . laugh . . . when . . . you . . . look . . . at . . . your . . . waistline." Yes, yes, yes, yes, yes!

"Women . . . know . . . when . . . the . . . soup . . . is . . . done." Yes, yes, yes, yes, yes!

---

try this:

Teach the Proverbs game to some friends and play it around the dinner table. Enjoy your combined wisdom.

[the first maxim]

say yes

* Just say yes.

* Become a "can-do" person.

* Look for the positive spin, for what is right.

* Agree with those around you.

* Cultivate yes phrases: "You bet"; "You are right"; "I'm with you"; "Good idea"; etc.

* Substitute "Yes *and*" for "Yes *but*." Add something to build the conversation.

* Exercise the yes muscle. This builds optimism and hope.

[the second maxim]
don't prepare

Empty yourself of everything.

— LAO TSE, *Tao Te Ching*

give up planning. Clear your mind instead of filling it. Don't spend your energy in preparing for the future. Redirect it to the present moment. Instead of packing, show up empty-handed but alert, cheerful, and ready to receive unexpected gifts. Change the habit of getting ready for life in favor of getting on with it now.

We often substitute planning, ruminating, or list-making for actually doing something about our dreams. Hence, the Boy Scout motto, the insurance industry, and a world of to-do–list software. The habit of excessive planning impedes our ability to see what is actually in front of us. The mind that is occupied is missing the present.

No one is suggesting that open-heart surgery should be improvised. I want a surgeon who has performed the procedure before, studied the method, and succeeded a number of times. However, if my operation is not going according to formula, I certainly hope that my doctor is a good improviser. I hope that she can look with fresh eyes at what needs to be done.

Imagine a language class in which students sitting in rows are expected to translate a passage. It's natural to count ahead and figure out which sentences you will have to decipher when your turn comes. Your attention fixates on the material ahead, and you are missing what others are saying. Their data is critical to the context of the passage you will be translating, but you don't hear it. Experiments in social psychology have confirmed that we don't listen very well when we are going to be called on. Most participants had no memory of the names of those who introduced themselves just before or just after them. We are either preparing our own remarks or judging how well we did. Everyone does this to some extent—think ahead, when we ought to be listening.

To improvise, it is essential that we use the present moment efficiently. An instant of distraction—searching for a witty line, for example—robs us of our investment in what is actually happening. We need to know everything about *this* moment.

Instead of preparing an outcome, ready yourself for whatever may come. Open your eyes, breathe fully, and attend to just this moment. Make it your world. Allow planning or thinking-ahead thoughts to pass through if they occur. If your mind gets absorbed in these thoughts ("stockpiling," I call it), redirect your attention to a detail in the immediate environment. Just as stray thoughts occur in a meditation, allow planning thoughts to pass by like clouds. Don't go with them.

Substitute attention for preparation. Then you will be working in real time. Focusing attention on the present puts you in touch with a kind of natural wisdom. When you enter the moment with heightened awareness, what you need to do becomes obvious. You discover that you already have the answers. Each of us is full of images, words, solutions, advice, stories. Trust your imagination. Trust your mind. Allow yourself to be surprised. This way of working feels quite different from that of "thinking up an answer."

Or if the notion of not being prepared is simply too much, try substituting the idea "Be prepared to let go" or "Be ready to go wherever things are going." Cultivate a flexible mind that is ready to act.

---

try this:

Spend a day without a plan. Have an adventure. Instead of following ordinary routines at this time, open your eyes especially wide and move along with curiosity and attention. Don't consult your to-do list; instead decide what to do based on what needs to be done right now, using your heightened awareness.

Danielle sat in the weekly sales meeting daydreaming as her boss illustrated quarterly-earnings estimates with a slide show. Normally she used the presentation time to doodle on her legal pad, appearing to listen, but actually preparing her own remarks. Today was different, however. "Suppose I really pay attention to the information being presented," Danielle thought. She began to focus fully on the report, studying the graphs carefully. An interesting thing happened. She noticed a sales trend in her division and, piecing together this data, formulated a new idea about product development. When she did speak, the ideas were fresh and timely and grew out of what she had just observed.

try this:

Substitute Zen-like attention for planning.
When you notice that your mind is planning what you
will do or say, make a conscious shift of attention to the
present moment. Notice everything that is going on
now. Attend to what others are saying or doing as if you
would need to report it in detail to the CIA. Listen with
both ears. Substitute attention to what *is* happening for
attention to what *might* happen.

Imagine a box, beautifully wrapped, sitting in front of
you. Take a moment to "see" the box.

*What color is the paper and ribbon? Touch the package. Now pick up
the box and check the weight. Shake it, if you like. Now carefully open the
package, setting aside the wrapping. Open the lid and look inside.*

What's the first thing that you see?

Take out the gift and examine it.

Notice a detail about the object.

Thank the giver.

What did you find? Did you surprise yourself? Was this
exercise effortless, or did you freeze at some point? Perhaps
you "thought up" what should be in the box before you
opened it. This is like unwrapping a gift that you packed
yourself. Perhaps you didn't like what was in the box—you
were disappointed, so you quickly rejected that first image
and sought out a good idea. This may result in finding the
box empty at first. All of these control strategies are normal.
We are accustomed to taking responsibility for the content
of our world, and so we "think up" something to put in the

box. Isn't that what we are supposed to do? Don't we have to come up with an idea?

No. Relax. You don't need to do anything at all. Trust that the gift is already there. Then discover what it is.

There is always something in the box—reality puts it there. How can this be? Where do ideas come from? In the West we view the individual as the creator. Works of art represent the mind of the artist, who takes credit or blame for them. Artists are put on a pedestal. It is little wonder that most of us don't see ourselves as gifted in this way and avoid expressing anything. However, Eastern notions of art characterize this relationship between the artist and the work quite differently. The artist is considered the servant of the muses, not their master. The artist shows up, practices carefully the strokes or steps, and then humbly takes his place as channel, as shepherd for the images to be brought forth. Ideas, songs, poems, paintings *come through* the individual but are not thought to be *of* him. On Bali everyone is considered an artist. Art is simply what one does, not who one is.

A famous Japanese Noh actor told me that his preparation for public performance involved a quiet meditation that was focused on becoming empty. He was attempting to set aside his attachment to self or personal consciousness. Once he had attained this opening or sense of spaciousness, the spirit of the role could enter his body and use him to fulfill its purpose. How different this is from the Western actor's habit of psyching himself into the character, of filling up with intention and motivation.

The second maxim's advice, "Don't prepare," really means to let go of our ego involvement in the process. When we give up the struggle to show off our talent, a natural wisdom can emerge; our muses can speak through us. All of our past experience, all that we have ever known, prepares us for this moment. We are overflowing with images, ideas, words, thoughts, and dreams. The trick is to stop choosing and to welcome what is there. Allow yourself to be surprised. Accept what you see completely. Finally, beyond acceptance is appreciation and thanks. For the improviser there are no wrong answers or bad gifts.

While we can't control what we find inside the box, we can always control our response to it. Discover what is right, what is interesting, what is useful about the gift that appears to you. Avoid expressing disapproval. Be a gracious receiver. When we train our minds to accept whatever arises, ideas grow, and we nourish the garden of our imagination. If the judge or the critic shows up offering advice, simply redirect him to the punch bowl in the corner, with appreciation. These fellows mean well, but they are unwanted guests at the beginning of the creative process.

Do the exercise once more. See a beautifully wrapped gift in front of you now. Pick it up and open it. Allow yourself to be surprised, interested in whatever appears. Substitute acceptance for judgment.

Coping with Fear

Suppose you are afraid that your box will be empty or that words will not come when you need to speak? Shouldn't you deal with this problem first? Don't improvisers need confidence to begin?

Fortunately, they do not.

Cara Alter, a San Francisco business consultant, suggests "putting on your coat of confidence—physically," as if it were an actual coat. She demonstrates grabbing an imaginary overcoat and slipping into it. When she does this, her posture improves and she stands taller. I suspect that this adjustment is actually the key for her. But affirmations or techniques don't always work.

I'm a professional. Students tell me that I appear self-assured in front of a class. They are surprised to learn that after more than forty years on stage and in the classroom, I still experience anxiety and classic signs of stage fright before I teach. I rarely sleep well before a presentation; I am often awake much of the night, worrying and spinning nightmarish scenarios. I want to be liked, and I fear failure and disapproval. No matter how many accolades I have received, I still imagine that my teaching or my public speaking won't be good enough. The specter of displeased critics has a permanent place in my imagination.

Thousands of successful public presentations have not dispelled this fundamental dread. If I experience confidence it is usually *after* the performance or class. "Confidence follows success"[2] is what I have learned. What does this tell us about handling stage fright and its attendant negative thoughts? Trying to overcome this fear is the wrong strategy. There isn't any need to fix these feelings. (Most of us want to, however.) Not only are they natural and universal, but they show how much we want to succeed. In the center of our anxiety is the seed of the desire to achieve, to do well. While stage fright isn't pleasant, it is manageable if we don't give it authority.

Performance anxiety comes from excessive self-focus. "Everyone is looking at *me*. I am not good enough. What if I fail? What will everyone think of me if I make a mistake?" The ego takes the stage and holds court. This line of thinking is misguided, anyway. *They* want you to succeed, to do well. Rarely are you being judged. It is more likely that *they* are cheering for you and tolerant of mistakes or miscues.

What is the improv fix for sweaty palms and a frozen mind? First of all, don't believe the voice that tells you that you "can't" do anything. The notion that you are actually paralyzed by fear is a lie. You can move. You can change what you are doing. If you are standing, try sitting; if you are sitting, move around. Redirect your attention from the symptoms to something constructive. Don't fight the fear or attend to it. That simply fuels it. Notice and accept whatever you feel, and turn your attention to doing something useful. If tears fill your eyes, wipe them with a tissue. Look over your notes. Focus on the sheet music. Stir the paints. See who is in the audience; name them or learn their names, if you can. Notice what each is wearing. Look around to see what others are doing. Ask someone a question. Count the number of people who are helping and supporting you; consider their contributions. Observe the room, its furnishings, the lighting sources, your materials. Breathe consciously. Smile. Laugh. Keep moving.

Changing your focus can provide relief. And even if the sweaty palms persist, your attention is where it is needed — on what you are doing. Thus, performance anxiety can be understood as a matter of self-absorption, of misplaced attention, and the remedy lies in turning your attention to the act of doing whatever it is — well. (Or, if doing it *well* seems a stretch at that moment, then do it adequately or even poorly, but do it.) Think about your purpose instead. Fear is not the problem; allowing your attention to be consumed by it is.

Indian Buddhist writer Vasubandhu pointed out the five universal human fears:[3]

1. Fear of death
2. Fear of loss of income
3. Fear of loss of reputation
4. Fear of loss of consciousness
5. Fear of speaking in front of people

Vasubandhu knew that stage fright is right up there with our fundamental fear of dying. So, as improvisers, we notice our fear, and just get on with the improvisation. No big deal.

Rachel, a shy student, offered this testimonial. "My aunt Rebecca had been a mentor. Her death, at a relatively young age, was unexpected. I was sad sitting at her funeral, but I recognized it as an important time for honoring her life. So, when the rabbi said: 'And now if there is anyone who would like to speak about Rebecca, please come forward,' I was surprised to observe myself rise and walk to the podium. Although my heart was beating fast and my balance was shaky, I was able to address the congregation. Full of love for Rebecca, I found myself improvising a warm testimonial about her wisdom and kindness. Words came. It may not have been a perfect speech, but it was heartfelt. I am so grateful that I didn't let my fear get in the way of what I needed to do. It would have been a real loss to miss that opportunity. Afterwards, many friends came up to me and thanked me for speaking."

Are there times when you have avoided speaking because you thought that you lacked preparation or didn't know which words to use? When the human heart has something to say, saying it is always timely. Improvisers always speak without a plan. Discover the freedom that comes when you trust that you have what you need. Remember, *there is always something in the box.*

[the second maxim]
don't prepare

* Give up planning. Drop the habit of thinking
  ahead.
* Attend carefully to what is happening right now.
* Allow yourself to be surprised.
* Stockpiling ideas for future use is unnecessary.
* Trust your imagination. There is always something
  in the box.
* Welcome whatever floats into your mind.
* Fear is a matter of misplaced attention. Focus on
  redirecting it.

[the third maxim]
just show up

Stop talking. Start walking.

—L. M. HEROUX

this principle is deceptively simple: Just show up. *Where* we are makes a difference. Move your body toward your dreams—to where they're happening—the gym, the office, the yoga class, your kitchen, the improv class, the garage, a cruise ship, the word processor, the construction site, the senior center, the theater. You know where. Be there physically. With the advent of cell phones you may have noticed that the time-honored greeting "How are you?" has been replaced by the query "Where are you?" Location means everything.

It's surprising how powerful the third maxim is. How often we avoid showing up for the things we need to do in life. Procrastination, laziness, fears—it's easy to find a reason for not going. The "just" in this maxim reminds us that showing up is already enough. Woody Allen quipped that it is "eighty percent of success." Prerequisites such as motivation, desire, and warm, fuzzy feelings aren't necessary. It is a con to imagine you must have these to get going. Improvisers know this. If they had to wait for inspiration or a good idea, few scenes would ever begin. Players step onto the stage because that is where things are happening. They just show up. Then the magic begins.

Kick-start your life—walk, run, crawl, fly, bicycle; move in the direction of your purpose. Love your parents? Pay them a visit. Need to write? Sit down at your desk. Want to have more friends? Show up at a volunteer job or a class in a subject that interests you. Need to exercise? Go to the gym or walk to the park. Believe in ecology? Take a plastic bag to the neighborhood park and pick up trash.

When you show up it is important to be on time. The issue of punctuality is critical when the activity is a shared one. Every minute counts. Each latecomer robs the whole group of time to work together. Taking time seriously shows courtesy. You are part of a greater picture that includes everyone with whom you share a purpose. Showing up for class on time, I tell my students, is their first big step in becoming an improviser.

Timeliness applies equally to couples, families, and companies. And don't forget to be on time when you are by yourself. Treat your own time as valuable. Benjamin Franklin reminds us that "time lost is never found again."

Using Rituals

Why not jump-start the process of showing up by using a ritual? Daily rites that precede the main event can be powerful triggers. These may involve putting on special clothing or equipment, going to a specific location, organizing the work area, or cleaning the space. In her enlightening book *The Creative Habit,* celebrated choreographer Twyla Tharp confesses that her ritual at 5:30 each morning is putting on leg warmers, going out onto the sidewalk in front of her New York apartment, and hailing a taxi to take her to her uptown workout studio. The moment that she steps into the taxi her day is on the right track.

A busy litigator joked that his ritual was stepping into the shower. Once he had gotten his body behind the glass and under the steaming hot water, his day was under way, on track. On mornings when he hung around sipping coffee and debating how to spend the day, he was more likely to waste time and lose direction. For him, stepping into the shower began a sequence of positive actions that effectively launched his day. Even on the weekend, stepping into the shower had the payoff of setting his course.

For me, it is making the bed. Every morning as soon as my body is standing I make the bed. I smooth the sheets, pull the blankets tight, tucking them under the mattress, arrange the patchwork quilt over the bedding, place the nine pillows (some functional, some decorative) into studied casualness, and fold a throw onto the bottom of the bed. This takes less than two minutes. When my husband and I get up at the same time, we do this together as one of many happy rituals of married life. Once the bed is dressed, the room feels orderly, and, for me, normal. Now the day begins. I am astonished by the number of people who find this ritual unnecessary. "Why on earth make the bed, since you are just going to get back in it at night?" I recommend it, however. Perhaps you already have a ritual that puts you on course. What is it?

I first experienced using preparatory rituals in 1980, in a village outside Kyoto where I went to study the Japanese arts. The program, sponsored by the Oomoto School of Traditional Japanese Arts (Oomoto is a Shinto sect, which has been called one of the new religions of Japan), was introducing a small group of foreigners to the art of tea ceremony, calligraphy, martial art, and Noh drama. Their faith has the unusual tenet "Art is the mother of religion," and they believe that an individual can become a better person by engaging in these ancient forms, which require sacrifice, precision, and attention. Each art is considered a *way* (*do* in Japanese): Cha*do* (the way of tea), Sho*do* (the way of the brush), Bu*do* (the way of the sword), and the *shimai,* or "dance," of Noh drama. We studied each of these subjects every day for a month. Classes rotated for variety, and the schedule included special visits to the Urasenke Tea School in Kyoto, and the pottery studios of Bizen artists. The program was designed to be hands-on, a practical introduction to the deep mysteries of the arts we studied. We were offered the opportunity to wear a kimono and wield a tea scoop, a fan, a sword, and a brush.

Each class began with the ritual of cleaning or preparing ourselves to begin the practice. In the Budo hall, students wiped the floor spotlessly clean by pushing cotton cloths over the tatami, becoming human street sweepers—outstretched arms propelling the rags along the sweet-smelling mats. On the polished wooden floor of the Noh stage, we did the same cleaning ritual as in the Budo hall—bending forward, our butts in the air in a funny triangle pose, pressing our weight along the floor, and pushing the cloths. At our desks in calligraphy class, we began with the ritual of grinding the ink. There is a correct way to hold the ink stick and to move it in small circles in a tiny pool of water on the stone that serves as an inkwell. The action of making ink became both a physical and mental preparation for the work of learning how to paint Japanese characters and bamboo leaves.

These rituals at the beginning of each session had the effect of creating order and harmony. We knew what we had to do when we entered the space. Cleaning, and grinding ink, got us into the world of the art without the stress of creation. There was a calming effect (just cleaning, I can do this).

These rituals were simple ways to show up; they provided stability. Ironically, stability is a vital element when we improvise.

---

try this:

Create a simple ritual. Identify a habit that you wish you had. (Exercising, reading regularly, meditating, paying bills.) Think of what will make the habit easy or more attractive to do. (Shall I lay out clothing or equipment, clean or organize my desk or workplace?) Set a time to do the preparatory ritual each day. Focus on doing it faithfully.

Showing Up for Others

Showing up is the key principle when we offer service to others. So often it is our presence alone, rather than some special ability, that makes the difference. Ian, a lanky improviser, had volunteered on Wednesday afternoons to be a tutor for underprivileged fifth-graders at the East Palo Alto children's center. He confided his doubts about having what it would take to be a mentor. However, he discovered that all he really needed to do was to show up on time, and good things happened. Ian's presence in the life of his students was the critical element. Is there someone you could be helping by showing up?

Edward's father was in a nursing home. He knew that it was important to visit his dad, but his mind was skillful at creating reasons for avoiding the trip. Something else always demanded his attention, and that right time to drop in never seemed to materialize. One Saturday morning, setting aside the mental chatter about whether to go, Edward just got out of bed, put on his clothes, and drove to the Martha Jefferson Nursing Home. After that he started showing up first thing every Saturday morning. The hours filled with simple, everyday conversations were meaningful to them both. Edward's life improved when he got his body to the place where his heart knew he ought to be. Three months later, when his father passed away, Edward understood the wisdom of "just showing up." Don't wait for a convenient time to do those things that are important to you.

---

try this:

Just show up. Make a list of five places that are your "hot spots," places where the important things in life happen for you. Why not put the book down, pick one of the places on your list, and show up there?

Changing Location

Once we have gotten where we need to be, how do we maximize our experience? How do I keep on showing up once I'm there? Sometimes we are in the right place physically, but we have somehow gone to sleep. At these times I recommend random change.

A very simple technique, which can have surprising benefits, involves changing physical location. During my workshops and classes, I ask students several times each hour to "change where you are in the room." Everyone gets up, shuffles around, and reorganizes themselves into a new pattern. As we move around seeking new locations within the same room, we help our minds to stay alert and avoid getting stuck in a rut. It is a good practice in letting go of attachment to our preferences as well. I remind students at the beginning of class to "find a new place or different vantage point in the circle when we stand." We all know that habit is a great deadener. Simply changing *where* we do things can have a positive effect. Remember what a delight it was when a teacher said: "Let's go outside today and have class under the big oak tree"? Just moving outside seemed mischievous, didn't it?

My friend artist Josephine Landor taught me how to apply the random-change principle in life. She had a way of making the simplest activities, like having lunch together, into a grand adventure, a serendipity. Her getaway cottage in Kenwood, California, was our school. Each day we stayed there, she would arrange a new setting for our meals. If the sun was hot over by the porch, we would move the picnic table across the yard near the bamboo grove. Or, to catch the best glimpse of the rising moon, we might set up the table on the back deck near the cypress trees. It seems we were always moving that picnic table. Josephine knew how to look at the environment and take advantage of the nicest perspective. These changes were precious improvisations, which capitalized on the beauty of each moment.

try this:

Change the location of a familiar activity. Surprise your cohorts by moving the weekly meeting outdoors, to the booth of a coffee bar, to the lounge at a local museum. Try moving a chair into the garden to read a book. Take your lunch to a new location away from your workplace. Explore a new vantage point.

[the third maxim]
just show up

* Walk, run, bike, skip to the places that you need to be.
* Motivation is not a prerequisite for showing up.
* Start your day with what is important.
* Use rituals to get things going.
* Showing up to help others is already service.
* Change your vantage point and refresh your mind.
* Location, location, location—in real estate and in life.
* Be on time for the sake of others.
* Show up on time for yourself. Lost time is never found.

[the fourth maxim]
start anywhere

How lovely to think that no one need wait a moment; we can start now, start slowly changing the world! How lovely that everyone, great and small, can make their contribution toward introducing justice straightaway. . . . And you can always, always give something, even if it is only kindness!

— *The Diary of Anne Frank*

The professional improv actors of San Francisco's 3 For All start each of their stories by asking for a simple suggestion from the audience. Quickly fielding a word or phrase from the chaos of shouts, Rafe, Tim, and Steve begin the scene without hesitation. They understand this vital improv principle: All starting points are equally valid. They begin where they are, often in the middle.

There's no need to find the right starting place. With a big task or a confusing problem, when you don't know where to start, begin with the most obvious thing, whatever is in front of you. The notion that there is such a thing as a *proper* beginning, and the search to find that ideal starting place, robs us of time. We distance ourselves from the task, and the vision of what it will take to do it makes tackling the job seem mountainous. Once a job is under way you have a new and more realistic perspective. You are inside the problem while looking at it, rather than standing safely at the perimeter. The Start Anywhere rule is liberating. It means that you can begin to make progress on some dream or dreaded task at any time.

Years ago I helped Mary, an improviser who was also a housewife. She was overcome with the clutter generated by her two small children. She reported that her house was "a disaster zone." Her mother had been a perfect housekeeper, and Mary found herself making comparisons. She obsessed over the thought that she'd never be as good as her mom. There were dirty dishes, toys on the floor, shopping to do, trash to empty, and all the ordinary tasks of running a household. Mary looked around at the disorderly scene and day by day became more depressed. "I don't know where to begin," she moaned. So instead of doing anything she sat amid the growing pile, feeling like a failure. Is there a great pile of something in your life waiting for your attention and action?

I volunteered to come to her home (the third maxim: just show up), since sitting and talking in my classroom struck me as a poor way to solve the problem. Once she knew that I was coming, she began to clean up, and when I arrived she showed me the mess with a mixture of angst and pride: "See, I told you it was awful." As I walked along the hall to her kitchen, I picked up stray toys, placing them in a playpen. Once in the kitchen, I started cleaning as I talked. "Just look around and do what seems obvious to you," I said, loading sticky cereal bowls into the dishwasher. Mary began picking up newspapers, cleaning, dumping things in the trash, putting a milk carton in the refrigerator. We continued talking as we cleaned and organized whatever was in front of us. In less than twenty minutes the kitchen was under control and we moved to the living room, dealing with the next most obvious thing and then the next. By the end of our hour together, much of the basic housework had been done. There was an encouraging sense of space throughout the house.

---

try this:

Start anywhere. Identify a project or task that needs to be done. When you put this book down, follow your first thought and begin the job. Do the very first thing that comes to mind. Continue doing what comes next.

This fourth maxim also applies to speech. To respond to a question or start improvised scenes, begin immediately using the first words that come to you. Trust your mind. Your first thought is a reasonable starting place; it is good enough. Don't hesitate. Once you begin speaking, you have something to work with and build on. With the first-thought method it is as if the idea selects you rather than the other way around. The improviser focuses on making that idea into a good one, rather than searching for a "good idea."

Judgment, preferences, and the filter of values can quickly crowd out first thoughts. The tree outside my window is no longer just a tree; it becomes "a redwood that is blocking my view of the ocean, a reminder of a thoughtless neighbor who lets plants run wild, and an obstacle to my concentration." We are clever at rejecting first thoughts. "That is uninspired or boring"; "I don't like it", "It is too revealing"; "Somebody else already said that"; "I'm afraid of where this will lead." It is easy to build roadblocks for whatever your mind generates. Don't give in to this. Seize that precious first thought and honor it. Soon this way of working will become natural to you.

Writers write to discover what they have to say, bringing to consciousness what they already know. It is the same with speech: speak to discover what you want to say. Sculpt, correct, refine, and redirect your thoughts on the fly as you speak. Authentic speech includes lively editing as part of the process.

Valuing Improvised Speech

When he learned that I was teaching students to improvise, a San Jose State University professor of business remarked: "That seems to me to be the problem rather than the solution. Today, students just want to substitute bull for taking the time to prepare their remarks. I tell my students, 'You've gotta have a script.' Interviews are too important to be left to shooting the breeze."

While I understood his point, I don't think he understood what I mean by improvising. Improvising what we have to say, which engages us in real time, fitting the answer to the question, is never "bull." It is speech that is *to the purpose* instead of being "scripted." The problem with a script is that you are in a double bind. First, you may fumble the text or forget the exact wording, which creates hesitancy (forty years of watching actors struggle to remember their lines supports this), and second, if you are *delivering the script* you may not be answering the question. Think of politicians who reply with a prepared script no matter what question is asked.

To improvise is to create order out of chaos. It is more of an engineering job than an artistic one. When I speak spontaneously I am creating an answer that has meaning now.

While the language itself may lack the precision of an edited reply, the value lies in its freshness and authenticity. We all know what a canned lecture sounds like. Real speech (improvised speech) will always be more interesting, attention-getting, and persuasive than its scripted sister.

You can improve how you give a lecture by using the principle of improvised speech. Instead of writing out your notes in precise language, try writing *questions* to yourself. Then, answer the question using natural speech patterns. Here are two examples of speech notes.

SCRIPTED:

I want to thank Mr. Whizup for inviting me to speak to the Rotary today. I'd like to begin by telling you how I got started teaching improvisation. The year was 1979, and I was a student of tai chi. My tai chi master, Chungliang Al Huang, invited Professor Keith Johnstone, a Canadian improv teacher, to join him in a workshop. As a drama teacher I was particularly interested in Johnstone's ideas. Subsequently, I began teaching his games and theories to my acting classes at Stanford. Students loved the games and seemed to find a kind of freedom in this approach to acting.

IMPROVISED NOTES:

1. Who invited me to be here? Whom shall I thank?
2. Who introduced me to improvisation? When?
3. When did I first teach improv?
4. Why was improv especially useful at Stanford?

Using the question method, I am free to add and develop details that fit the moment. When I use the scripted text it

becomes difficult to add anything. I naturally focus on reading
the prepared text well. However, when I am answering a question, using the second method, my mind becomes active in organizing information in real time. The result is more natural.

Decades ago when I was a graduate student at Wayne
State University, I took four classes in what was then called
oral interpretation. Each class focused on a subject area: the
oral interpretation of prose, poetry, the Bible, and Shake-
speare. I expected to learn a variety of techniques to handle
the differences in literary style. Instead, class after class the
professor gave only one instruction: "Talk to me"; "Talk to me
with that poem"; "Talk to me with that passage from Isaiah";
"Talk to me with that sonnet"; "Just talk to me, please."
Whenever a student's speech had the sound of declamation or
rhetoric, Professor Skinner would stop and kindly remind
him: "No need to make this an oration; just talk to me with it."

That was no small feat. The sound of someone talking is
natural and communicative. The sound of reading is something else entirely. Only the most highly trained actors can
turn scripted words into natural-sounding speech. Instead,
speak off the cuff. Trust your mind.

try this:

Improvise a short monologue now. Compose
your thoughts as you go along. Don't hesitate. Use one
of these topics:

"If there were four more hours in the day, how
would you spend them?"

or

"Talk about something beautiful you saw recently."

[the fourth maxim]
start anywhere

* All starting points are equally valid.
* Begin with what seems obvious.
* Once it is under way any task seems smaller.
* When speaking in public don't use a script. Write down questions and answer them.
* Talk to your audience. Don't give a lecture.
* Trust your mind.
* Edit and develop ideas *as* you speak.

[the fifth maxim]
be average

When I told some New Yorkers about dumbness in a workshop two months ago, they were so relieved. They were tired of being alert and intelligent. They wanted dream time. Walk around your neighborhood dumb for a half hour.

—NATALIE GOLDBERG,
The Essential Writer's Notebook

Gene DeSmidt, a Bay Area builder, country musician, and Zen student, says that his construction company's motto is "Perfect is close enough." His reputation as a craftsman who cares is well known. When he built his own getaway cabin in northern California he quips that the line became "Close enough is perfect." This makes a lot of sense. The pictures of Gene's river house show that his "close enough" is actually terrific. I'll bet that yours is, too.

Giving it all you've got commonly backfires. There is a paradox that when we are trying hard the result is often disappointing. A healthier climate is one in which we tell ourselves to just be average. Take the pressure off. Avoid the mind-set that says "This one better be good!" or "Be original."

When you try hard to do your best, the effect on your performance is often to jinx it. In all cases there is something to lose. This can provoke tension and easily lead to anxiety. Instead, try the following advice:

"Dare to be dull." (Keith Johnstone)
"Be nothing special." (David K. Reynolds)
"Cultivate ordinary mind." (a Zen saying)

This rule may seem simplistic, but don't underestimate how well it works. Changing expectations can take the pressure off and may even cheer you up. *Radical Presence* author Mary Rose O'Reilley gives this example of deflecting perfection anxiety: "The poet William Stafford used to rise every morning at four and write a poem. Somebody said to him, 'But surely you can't write a good poem every day, Bill. What happens then?' 'Oh,' he said, 'then I lower my standards.' Three great lessons here—practice your art every day, lower your standards, and claim a time or place or an attitude that will challenge your bourgeois idea of reality. Four A.M.!"[4]

Samuel, a financial analyst, found this maxim to be his salvation. "You know, I've been torturing myself for years—overworking my research, pulling all-nighters, doing reports to a standard that I see now was simply obsessive. I never seemed to finish anything, since I was always trying to make it perfect. Your suggestion to be average was a revelation. Now I do the work, but I stop short of worrying it to death. And, the results are really just fine. I'm getting a lot more done."

The 2003 NFC playoff game was determined by the toss of the ball for a field goal. Everything hung on this play. Trey Junkin, the center for the New York Giants, who fumbled it, making the easy field goal impossible for the kicker, was quoted in the *San Francisco Chronicle* sports page as saying, "I tried to make a perfect snap when all I needed to do was make a good one." If he'd just snapped the ball normally, instead of trying to do it perfectly, the NFC championship, and perhaps the Super Bowl, might well have been won by New York.

Giving up on perfection is the first step; the next is to stop trying to come up with something different. Striving for an original idea takes us away from our everyday intelligence, and it can actually block access to the creative process. There is a widespread belief that thinking "outside the box" (some call this the goal of creativity) means going after far-out and unusual ideas. A true understanding of this phrase means seeing what is really obvious, but, up until then, unseen. "The real voyage of discovery lies not in seeking new landscapes but in having new eyes," said Marcel Proust.

Looking for the obvious offers us a way to approach problems that appear daunting. Trick yourself by turning a challenge into an ordinary task. "Anyone can walk a plank, but if it stretched across an abyss, fear might glue us to it. Our best strategy might be to treat the abyss as something ordinary (if that were possible) and to walk across in our average manner," wrote Keith Johnstone.

Do what is natural, what is easy, what is apparent to you. Your unique view will be a revelation to someone else. Remember the exercise in which you opened the box and discovered what was there? When I do this with twenty-five students, all opening the same-sized imaginary shoe box, the results are fascinating. Usually there are twenty-five distinctly different gifts: a snow globe, a brick, a deck of playing cards, a wooden flute, a live mouse, a package of coffee filters, a diamond necklace, a hand-knit sweater, a pile of old coins, running shoes, seashells, used CDs, lots of packing bubbles with a plastic toy whistle, a baby kitten, three hard-boiled eggs, a flashlight, etc. Occasionally more than one student finds the same object, but even when this happens the two watches found are different in design or make. When asked to uncover what is obvious to you, count on the fact that your view is already unique. Ingrid Bergman understood this point when she quipped, "Be yourself. The world worships the original."

Aaron, a software designer, shared this insight: "I used to censor many of my ideas before discovering a useful one. Now I look for the obvious in designing user interfaces for my product. When I go to meetings with Development and state what seems most readily apparent to me, the design executives slap their heads and say, 'Why didn't we think of that?'—which is when I know I have a good idea. Before, I often searched for something clever or innovative—missing what was right in front of me. This maxim [seeing the obvious] really makes sense."

Try thinking *inside* the box. Look more carefully.

This practice applies to speech as well. Say what you want to say in the way that seems natural to you. My paternal grandmother, Juliette Bethel Ryan, was a natural improviser. Once while fingering the obituary page and solemnly shaking her head, she sighed and said: "People are dying today that have never died before." Granny looked up, completely surprised by our laughter. It has been more than fifty years, but I still can hear her enthusiastic response when I told her that I had begun attending Sunday Quaker worship services. "Oh, those Quakers—wonderful, wonderful people, they are. Why don't they preach what they practice?" She embodied the spontaneous life, always finding the agreeable answer, the supportive remark. Her genius was in express-ing ideas just as she saw them.

It is inescapable: each of us sees the world in a different way. We need only to trust that our vantage point is worthy and give up striving after the original. You are.

---

try this:

Do it naturally. If there is something important that you need to do, approach the problem as though you didn't need to do your best. What is the most obvious way of solving it? How would you proceed if finding a solution was "nothing special?"

---

try this:

Consider ordinary gifts. Looking for a gift for a friend or loved one? Think of items that you use every day (a pillow for the bed, a cereal bowl, a teacup, a towel, a pen, a clock, bedroom slippers, a blanket, a sharp kitchen knife, a calendar, good coffee). Keep lists of useful everyday objects for help in choosing a good gift.

Bowling with a Chicken

When members of my group, the Stanford Improvisors, scratched their heads looking for a clever idea for their first T-shirt design, someone shouted, "How about a picture of a chicken standing on a bowling ball?" During an improv per-formance for one of the dorms, a freshman had volunteered this "helpful" suggestion: "In a bowling alley with a chicken." We had asked the audience to fill in the blanks: "In a _____, with a _____." This improv game is a setup, which typically results in pairing odd bedfellows. You almost always get "in a firehouse with a wildebeest" or "in a rowboat with a broken toaster oven." These suggestions arise from two assumptions, one of them mistaken. The first is that all we are here to see is comedy, and the second, that pairing "unlikely" objects will produce the biggest challenge and result in the funniest scene.

In several decades of watching improv shows, I've never once heard anyone shout: "In a bathtub with a rubber duck" or "In an office with a typewriter." No one wants to be thought unimaginative. The audience believes that ideas that seem ordinary or that "make sense" reflect a lack of creativity. I call it "the fallacy of the fried mermaid." When improvisers ask for a suggestion, an audience member will usually scream something like "fried mermaid." Everyone laughs, of course, since the weird juxtaposition of adjective and noun has already produced the humor. You can hear the buddies of the fellow who yelled it congratulating him on his wit. It is a closed loop, however. The joke is already over. Doing an actual scene about a fried mermaid isn't likely to result in a very appealing story, if you think about it.

Don't fall for the idea that something needs to be "way out" or whimsical to be creative. Getting a laugh is easy—trivial, actually. Anything unexpected seems funny. This kind of humor is like a sugar hit. It gives a temporary lift, but it is a poor diet and won't nourish artistically. If you give up making jokes and concentrate on making sense, the result is often genuinely mirthful. Besides, making sense is a lot more satisfying in the long run. Give the obvious a try.

[the fifth maxim]
be average

* Close enough is perfect.
* Dare to be dull.
* Think "inside" the box.
* Celebrate the obvious.
* What is ordinary to you is often a revelation to others.
* Remember "classics" or "favorites" can be fresh ideas, too.
* Don't make jokes. Make sense.

pay attention

If I have made any valuable discoveries, it has been owing more to patient attention than to any other talent.

—SIR ISAAC NEWTON

how are your powers of observation? How much do you notice and remember? This skill is at the heart of all improvising. What we notice *becomes* our world. So observe what is going on around you. Open your eyes, and notice the detail. See what is actually happening. Pay attention to everything.

One of the oldest Zen stories is about the student who climbs a tall mountain to ask the wise man the meaning of life. He replies that there are three secrets. The first is attention. And, to make a long story short, after two more laborious trips to the top, the student learns that secret number two and secret number three are also attention.

Our quality of life is directly tied to the sixth maxim. Life *is* attention, and what we are attending to determines to a great extent how we experience the world. We are usually focused on ourselves— our problems, desires, fears. We move through life half awake and ruminating, living in our heads—thinking, planning, worrying, imagining. The detail of each day takes place in front of us, moment by precious moment. How much are we missing? Almost everything.

What was the first thing you did this morning after getting out of bed? What items are sitting on the kitchen counter? Who was the last person you spoke to? Can you recall her words? What was that person wearing? Describe what you did yesterday from the time you woke up until you went to bed in the order in which it happened. A trained improviser could probably answer all of these questions. Can you?

try this:

How good is your attention? Please keep your eyes on *this* paragraph and keep reading until you come to the instruction "Close your eyes." Once your eyes are shut, *describe in as much detail as you can the immediate environment.* Don't cheat by glancing around now or studying the room with the assignment in mind. When your eyes are closed, *point to specific objects in the room. Describe colors, shapes, and the layout of the room; include as many details as you can remember.* Continue with your eyes closed until you can't think of anything else to report. When you have remembered all you can, open your eyes.

Now, close your eyes.

How did your description match reality? What obvious items did you overlook? What surprised you when you opened your eyes?

Look at your surroundings. Find three things you had not noticed before. Reality is rich in texture, color, and information. If you are good at observation, this exercise may help you see more of the detail. If you failed to notice very much, this exercise can stimulate you to observe more carefully.

Were you wrong about some things? "I thought the clock was over the sofa"; "I could have sworn the carpet was blue." Perhaps your mind added details or created information about the room. Even this can be good news for the improviser—to discover that our minds often fill in the blanks where memory fails. You may want to do the exercise often, to see if your attention improves.

Domingo, an energetic twenty-year-old undergraduate, came back from Los Angeles, where he'd found an agent. He was hoping to be discovered as an actor. Domingo had an epiphany doing this attention exercise. He stayed after class one day to tell me: "Yesterday I woke up, and lying in bed I listened to the birds singing outside my window. I actually *heard the melody* that they sang. I noticed the leaves on the tree were newly sprouted, yellow-green. Life was happening all around me, and I was seeing it for the first time. It is as if I've been given new eyes. There is so much going on in the world that I had simply never noticed before. Waking up to the miracle of attention has been life-changing for me. Attention is everything."

Domingo's *aha!* came from a fundamental shift in perspective. Usually his mind was focused on himself; when he started looking outside himself, his experience blossomed. For those of us caught in a spiral of self-absorption and rumination, the redirection of attention outward can have a profound effect. *Where* we are looking makes a difference.

The improviser's lifeline is his attention. Those on stage often appear clever simply because they have been paying attention to what has been said and remember it when most of the audience has forgotten. This is the real magic of the art of improv. Remembering names is a case in point.

I train my students to make a special effort to learn names when they are first given. People are always telling me: "I'm just no good at names." "Balderdash," I reply. "You were accepted into Stanford; you have memorized the table of elements; you know dozens of phone numbers and passwords and song lyrics. It is simply a lie that you 'can't remember names.' You may not have made the effort, but it is wrong to imagine that you can't."

It is shocking to me that intelligent people behave as if name retention were a genetic trait that they failed to carry at birth, when it is simply a matter of attention and requires a little effort. Repeat a name several times out loud when you first hear it. Look directly and fully at the person. Check to be sure that you are pronouncing it properly and that you have coded it by observing the face of the person to whom it belongs. Write it down, if you have the chance. Say it silently as well as out loud. Be prepared to ask again. You may need several tries before it is fixed in your mind. You may experience an embarrassing moment if you need to ask again. Don't let this stand in your way. Most people are pleased that you care about their names. Make the decision to be a person who notices and remembers names, and then start learning them.

I began this practice many years ago in an effort to do something constructive and divert myself from first-day teaching jitters. I commonly taught as many as five classes in a quarter. On the first day I tried to learn the names of every student, and there were often as many as thirty per class. I asked all my students to do the same. Many rolled their eyes, but we worked on it together. At the end of that first session when someone volunteered to name everyone in the room and succeeded, I loved the applause that students gave one another. What is equally rewarding is to watch someone try and struggle with the task, perhaps naming only half of those present. Learning names starts a habit of mind that is critical to the improviser — noticing who else is in the room. Imagine knowing the names of half of your classmates on the first day! I received an e-mail from a physician who shared that "the most useful thing I learned in your class was that I am a person who can remember names. I had simply never tried." Making this effort can blossom into a valuable habit that will serve you all your life.

In an improv scene a player comes on stage with her arms raised, indicating that she has just scrubbed up. Her intern joins her and says, "Dr. Bradley, we are delivering twins, I hear?" "Yes, Mark. Mrs. Greenaway is primed and ready. Let's go." The actress playing the attending nurse now entering needs to know all three names; Dr. Bradley, the physician; Mark, the intern; and Mrs. Greenaway, the expectant mother. It is very kind to repeat names as soon as convenient. This is true in life. When you give your name, you can help by doing it clearly, and by repeating it in a generosity of spirit. If someone gets it wrong or forgets, help her.

A good practice is to keep an eye out for the name tags that employees wear. When you see a name tag, read it. Learn the name and use it out loud, if appropriate. It is common these days for a salesclerk to notice yours when you proffer a credit card, and address you politely with· "Thanks for shopping at Safeway, Mrs. Madson."

Today is a good day to start remembering names.

Cultivating Awareness

If a police officer quizzed you, could you remember details about the people you encounter on an ordinary day? With effort we can improve. Here are some exercises that you can think of as "attention calisthenics." Assign yourself one of these each day. Notice the results.

---

try this:

Attend to one thing at a time. Choose an ordinary activity (sorting laundry, eating lunch, brushing your hair) and pay attention *only* to what you are doing while you are doing it for the duration of the task. Avoid multitasking. If you are eating, simply eat. Avoid reading the paper, listening to the radio, or having a conversation. Reflect on the taste of the food, on who prepared it, and how it came to you. If you notice that your mind has wandered, bring it back to what you are doing.

This may sound simple, but it is a very challenging exercise. No one does this perfectly. Keep returning your attention to the task. You are flexing a powerful muscle. It will get stronger. As you return your attention again and again to what you are doing, you learn something about reality as well as the workings of your mind. Enjoy those moments when your attention is aligned with your actions. Some call this state mindfulness, an awareness of what is happening now. But even a Zen master does not live in a state of mindfulness at all times. Progress is what we are after.

Some art forms build in the idea of paying attention to

what is right in front of us. Those who study the Japanese tea ceremony learn the concept of "tea talk." Guests know that inside the teahouse one must speak only about what is inside the house. Even polite discussion of the news, social or political events, or personal issues is forbidden, including complaining about the heat or mentioning any discomfort. Instead, the guest is invited to pay attention to the detail of what is present at that moment—the scroll in the alcove, the flower in the vase, the kind of sweet that was chosen to be served along with the bitter, frothy green tea. What is spoken is meant to be a reminder of the unique character of the event. The tea saying *Ichi go, ichi ei* means "One time, one meeting." This particular gathering will never happen again. Live it now. Savor the detail.

---

try this:

Notice something new. Use this exercise when you are in a familiar environment or doing a routine task. See how many new things you can observe. What haven't you noticed that has been there all along? When you find something, examine it carefully. Repeat the exercise in the same location at other times. Invite yourself to "notice something new" each time you return to this place or do this task.

Total Listening

It's common to listen to others halfheartedly, especially to those we know well. Lazy listening habits abound. But you can change this.

try this:

Listen completely. Once a day devote your attention 100 percent to someone who is speaking to you. Focus completely on what is being said. Look at the person as you listen. If you notice your mind drifting, simply bracket your thoughts temporarily and return your attention to the speaker. Listen as if you needed to repeat what is being said in perfect detail. Observe how this effort pays off.

Or use Brenda Ueland's inspiring description of this exercise:

> *Try to learn tranquility, to live in the present a part of the time every day. Sometimes say to yourself: "Now. What is happening now? This friend is talking. I am quiet. There is endless time. I hear it, every word." Then suddenly, you begin to hear not only what people are saying, but what they are trying to say, and you sense the whole truth about them.*[5]

try this:

Go for a fifteen-minute walk in your neighborhood. Imagine you have just landed there from another planet. Use all five of the senses: sight, sound, touch, taste, and smell.

What surprises you about your environment? What is especially beautiful or noteworthy? What needs doing around here (picking up trash, replacing a fallen garbage-can lid, weeding, sweeping)?

try this:

Study other people. Become a secret anthropologist. Notice (and remember) names and faces. Check out what people are wearing. Listen to what they have to say. Observe what kind of day they seem to be having; discern their manner or their mood. Return to a familiar shop or place of business and discover something new about the workers. Learn something new every day about those closest to you.

Pop Quiz

What are the names of the three characters in the hospital sketch discussed earlier? Who was the physician? What is the name of the intern? Who was having the twins? Check your answers (page 71).

[the sixth maxim]
pay attention

* Life *is* attention.
* Notice everything, particularly the details.
* Become a detective.
* Shift your attention from yourself to others.
* Make an effort to remember names and faces.
* Keep on waking up.
* This moment happens only once. Treasure it.
* Avoid multitasking. Attend to one thing at a time.

face the facts

To achieve excellence, we must first understand the
reality of the everyday, with all its demands and potential
frustrations.

—MIHALY CSIKSZENTMIHALYI, *Finding Flow*

When Ilyssa and Jennifer bound onstage to begin an improvised story, they rely upon realistic interaction. If Jenn starts the scene by saying, "Nice dog you've got there," Ilyssa must reply, "Yes, he's a prizewinning Dalmatian. He loves to hunt," or something that supports the initial offer. Ilyssa's remark is a good one, since she not only accepts Jenn's offer, she builds upon it. Improvisers need to enter the same reality in order to work together effortlessly. They establish the facts of the scene and agree to accept things as they are—in short, they act realistically.

The seventh maxim follows from the cardinal principle of saying yes. First we say yes, and then we work with what has been given. Saying yes is like accepting the bite of apple that is being offered. Facing the facts implies that we chew on the apple, allowing it to nourish us. Use what is given. Build upon it.

The Japanese have a word for this rule: *arugamama*. It is the virtue of abiding with things as they are. It implies a realistic and responsive approach to life. It is essential in good improv and provides sensible advice for ordinary life. The most consistent road to unhappiness that I know comes from turning a blind eye to reality. We do this when we wish potato chips weren't fattening and eat them anyway, put off doing the bills just one more day, live an unhealthy lifestyle, fail to heed warnings on the label (or don't even read the label), or focus on our partner's shortcomings and spend time trying to talk him into doing things our way.

Wishing things were different (or that *I* was different) simply wastes time. The improviser can't afford unrealistic thinking. Instead, she builds bridges over rocky terrain and turns lemons into lemonade. She works with what is actually in front of her, setting aside the temptation to dwell on what it is not.

Meghan was a successful corporate lawyer. She had joined the improv class to hone her skills in the courtroom. One Monday night she stayed behind to ask my advice. "I don't know if improvisation has a cure for my problem," she began. "I'm just one of those procrastinators. You see, I'm always behind with my billing. Everyone is on my case about it; my law partner, my husband, even the clients are concerned when the bills are late. I need to get to the root of what is going on with this issue." Then she asked, "Why am I always sabotaging myself? What's the improv fix for this?"

Meghan was fighting reality. She disliked this part of the work and was allowing that to be an excuse for not doing what was necessary. Calling herself a procrastinator seemed to explain why she was dodging the situation. The billing work had to be done, whether she felt like it or not. She lost the role of procrastinator the moment she faced the facts and started the work of billing her clients.

Wishing others would change is another way we avoid facing reality. Other people's behavior often gets on my nerves. I long for them to behave differently. Usually they don't, of course. I need to accept these differences and get on with the show. Improvisers recognize the value of working with many styles of playing and set aside their impulse to try to change others.

Myron could best be described as dour. He rarely smiled, preferring a steely, penetrating gaze and a no-nonsense response to most situations. He was always on time; he volunteered often; but no one in our improv troupe liked playing in scenes with him. I think most members of the group wondered why I'd picked him to be a player in the first place. Several of them came to discuss "what to do about Myron." My suggestion was to work with him. Accept him as he is. Pay attention to him. Begin a story with him as the hero. Treat him with the same respect and cooperation you'd give an admired fellow player. In short, set aside your complaints about his personality, and work with the offers and ideas he does bring to the table. He is how he is.

It was fascinating to watch Myron respond to being treated well. He flourished, and members of the group quickly noticed the change. Dealing well with people we like is easy; the mark of a fine improviser is his ability to work skillfully, kindly, and respectfully with those with whom he has difficulty.

Sometimes I'm simply asleep to the facts. I cast a blind eye to situations that I find troublesome. Perhaps I stop getting on the scale to check my weight and wear only loose clothing. How easy it is to bypass the obvious. Facing the facts means to keep your eyes wide open.

try this:

Write down the facts. Identify an issue or a situation in your life that needs attention (some personal challenge or work issue). Write a detailed description of the issue, indicating what the facts are. Avoid judgment, critical comments, or discussing your emotions. Use simple, declarative sentences. Work to create an objective picture of the problem first.

Now, taking into account all the facts, what needs to be done? Propose a course of action, and spell out the steps you need to take. Then take that first step.

Here is an example written by Louise:

Statement of the facts: "Louise's Weight"

On April 23, 2004, my weight is 173 pounds. I am five foot seven and a half inches tall. My physician, Dr. Winston, informed me that the ideal weight for my height is 140–155. So, even given a conservative view, I am twenty pounds overweight. I can see that I have gained several pounds each year over the past ten years. This trend is very likely to continue unless I do something differently.

I am exercising three to four times a week, and I keep moderately active with housework and shopping. I love to cook and to eat. My diet, which includes many healthy foods, is also high in carbohydrates. I have not officially counted calories, fats, or carbohydrates. I eat desserts nearly every day. I eat several pieces of bread each day. My portions are medium to large in size. I snack between meals occasionally. Clearly my food intake exceeds my energy output.

Proposed course of action:

1. *For one week, keep track of calories—write them down.*
2. *Reduce calories by 500 to 600 a day.*
3. *Have dessert only twice a week*
4. *Follow this plan for one month and see what happens.*
5. *Begin this today.*

The facts of any problem emerge when we look at the details. Writing them down allows you to be your own counselor. Be sure to include a realistic action plan, and then follow your own advice. Facing facts can be the first step in making important changes in your life.

Embracing the Wobble

Improvising has much in common with riding a bicycle, surfing, or skiing. Things are not stable, linear, or predictable. The situation is always in flux. Our footing keeps changing. This approach may be uncomfortable or unsettling at first, and it is natural to seek out security.

Even if we succeed in finding solid ground for a while, we can depend on the fact that it will eventually change; rocky terrain is unavoidable and may even be the path to something wonderful. "We can count on chaos," I tell my students. American Zen writer Alan Watts, clearly an improviser in spirit, named one of his books *The Wisdom of Insecurity*. He knew that life is all about balancing, not about being balanced.

I've been working with a physiotherapist to strengthen my leg muscles, which have been weakened by chronic tendonitis. One of my daily exercises involves standing on one foot balancing on a half cylinder made of Styrofoam. The goal is to stand for a whole minute on the flat side of the disc, curved side down, balancing on one leg. My first attempts were completely unsuccessful. I couldn't seem to balance even for a moment without tipping over. So I began doing the exercise standing next to a doorframe to have something to hold on to. It was still difficult, but I could manage it. I proudly showed the therapist my solution, and she rolled her eyes and intoned, "No, no, no. I don't want you to make it easier. I want you to struggle. That's how the muscles will learn to heal. By stabilizing things you defeat the point of the exercise. Stay with the uncertainty, please. Really, it's *all about the struggle*."

In the act of balancing, we come alive. Sensations change moment by moment; sometimes we feel secure, sometimes precarious. In the long run we develop tolerance for instability. As we come to accept this insecurity as the norm, as our home ground, it becomes familiar and less frightening. We can stop trying to flee from the wobble. And sometimes this sense of being off balance is exhilarating and reminds us of the impermanence and fragility of life, nudging us to appreciate each imperfect, teetering moment we are alive. Perhaps, like surfers, we can come to feel the power of the waves, the majesty of the elements, and a sense of our own place in this swirling universe.

[the seventh maxim]
face the facts

* Don't fight reality.
* Accept other people as they are.
* Work with what you have been given.
* What *are* the facts? You are probably not noticing all of them.
* Embrace the wobble.
* Insecurity is normal. Count on it.

[the eighth maxim]
stay on course

God has given each of us our "marching orders." Our purpose here on Earth is to find those orders and carry them out. Those orders acknowledge our special gifts.
—SØREN KIERKEGAARD

a n improvisation always has a point. It is never simply "whatever." On stage we improvise in order to make a story together, to solve a puzzle, to create a new song, to bring delight to an audience. At home we improvise to fix a broken picture frame, to find the kindest way to make a suggestion, to help a neighbor, to honor a promise, to use leftovers creatively, to repair a friendship. At work we may improvise to meet a deadline, assuage a finicky boss, or solve a problem with limited resources.

Some guiding force underlies each moment. We need to keep in mind what we are aiming for. Instead of asking, "What do I feel like doing?" substitute "What is my purpose now?" The difference in the answer may be illuminating. We have become a culture in which "How do you feel?" is the most commonly asked question (by therapists, doctors, news reporters, etc.), as if our emotions were *the* most important thing in life. This is odd, since feelings are fleeting and temporal and certainly not always the wisest basis for our actions. Most definitions of the word "purpose" suggest a moral component. It can be seen as "the proper activity" for a person or "the right thing to be doing." It always implies conscious intention. Answering this question provides direction.

What is your purpose right now? Take a moment to think about this question. Perhaps you want to find strategies for living more spontaneously. Or, are you avoiding a difficult task by diverting yourself with reading? Or maybe you are a student of improvisation, hungry for clues to this magical art. Could it be that someone gave you this book and you are reading it to discover why it was given to you? Perhaps you are waiting for the clothes to dry and are simply filling time. The same activity may be driven by different reasons. Checking to see if you are still on target is sensible and provides guidance about whether to continue or change to some other activity.

During a holiday season, I found myself browsing the huge Hillsdale Mall, admiring the decorations and checking out the sales designed to lure customers. I was drawn into the lingerie department and began to wander the aisles, fingering the luxurious downy fabric of gowns and robes. I'm addicted to soft things, especially fleece, which I consider a modern-day gift from God. As I brushed my hand against the velvety nap of the fleece pajamas hanging in rows, I heard an interior voice say, "What's your purpose now, Patricia?" I remembered that I had come to the mall to find a present for my sister. Looking down, I saw the set of cake pans waiting to be wrapped, safely stowed in my shopping bag. My objective had been accomplished. The next thing to do was to drive home to my afternoon work, writing this chapter. This reminder was all I needed to turn from the rows of colorful clothing and make my way back to the car.

Sometimes, of course, my aim is recreation or simple delight, and I wander the brightly lit mall to enjoy the sights and stimulation and revel in the pleasures of soft green fleece pajamas. But it wasn't on this occasion.

The eighth maxim is useful as we navigate relationships in business and in our personal lives. Anna had been living with her partner, Allen, for seven years. Allen's architectural firm had offered him a promotion and a more interesting assignment if he would move to Atlanta. The couple had been arguing over the decision. Anna was upset that he was not considering her feelings in asking her to make the move. When she asked herself, "How do I feel about Allen?" a lot of resentment and disappointment came up. However, when she changed the question and asked, "What is my purpose in being with Allen?" a light dawned. The course she had set for herself was to build a supportive life together—one in which they each looked out for the welfare of the other. There was no compelling need for her to stay in Boalsburg. Of course she should support his move. Anna had lost sight of the reason that they were together. Remembering it at this time was a great relief.

Use the litmus of purpose when overwhelmed with feelings or confused about a decision. Objectives come in many sizes and shapes, and there is meaning in everything we do.

try this:

"**What is my purpose now?**" Use this question as a weathervane. Ask it often, especially when you are anxious or unsure of what to do next. When you have the answer, act upon it.

Finding Your Purpose

The question of purpose is an invitation to consider daily or short-term goals and intentions as well as larger aims. My life seems to run more smoothly when I stay on course. A successful writer I know has a typed card above his computer that states simply: "There is Reality's work that only you can do." The line has several meanings. From one perspective all useful work that I do serves others in some way. (I can't escape doing reality's work.) Another take on the line urges me to notice my particular gifts, talents, and location. What work has been given to me that is uniquely mine? *What would not get done if I were not here?* I can examine this question by observing the details of what is in my care. Naturally, family comes to mind. My roles as wife, as daughter, as aunt are uniquely "mine." Right now I am the only aunt to my nephew Nathan. Am I doing a good job as his aunt? Is there anything more I need to do?

Another way to answer the question is to check out talents and passions. What do I find easy to do? What seems natural? What do I do well? What do I love doing? Could it be that my preferences, natural abilities, and even my fascinations are all part of the answer to the question?

---

try this:

What would not get done if you were not here? Consider your unique vantage point, your talents, your loves, what you have been given to do. (If your first answer to this question is "It wouldn't make any difference to the world if I were not here," think again.) What are you here to do? If you keep a journal, pose this question and answer it in writing.

[the eighth maxim]
stay on course

* Every improvisation has a point.
* Don't let feelings alone run your show.
* There is meaning in everything we do, even small tasks.
* Keep an eye on where you are going.
* If you miss the target, adjust your aim.
* Ask often: "What is my purpose?"
* What would not get done if you were not here?

[the ninth maxim]
wake up to the gifts

One of the key principles of the Zen cook is that nothing exists by itself. Everything is interdependent.
—BERNARD GLASSMAN AND RICK FIELDS,
Instructions to the Cook

to the improv professional the glass is always half full. There is always something there to work with; you just need to see it. It is possible that your glass is already brimming with a delicious brew and that you are actually at a banquet. Everywhere you turn, something or someone is helping you. You may have been asleep to all this, however. Waking up can be illuminating. There are gifts everywhere if we learn to see them.

I am always using some kind of filter when I encounter the world, whether I notice this or not. The light in which something is perceived will determine its value. I can look at a person or event from three vantage points:

1. To see what's *wrong* with it (*the critical method*—commonly used in higher education). Using this lens the *self* looms large.
2. To see it objectively (*the scientific method*). Using this lens both the *self* as well as *others* are meant to disappear.

3. To see the *gift* in it (*the improviser's method*). With this lens *others* loom large.

How do you look at reality? Which lens do you use? My personal default is the critical method. I notice what's wrong or what bugs me about a situation. I know a lot about how other people cause me trouble or let me down. I have to use effort to set aside these prejudices in order to see things "objectively." Objectivity requires that I shift out of my egocentric view. Rarer still is the approach of contemplating the "gift" apparent in the moment. This takes a new kind of effort. The results can be astonishing, especially if you've never tried this before.

Our natural sense of entitlement can be an obstacle. If I experience something as *mine,* I won't see it as a gift. "I bought this chair; it is my property." Even in a public venue a sense of ownership often prevails. If I pick a seat in a movie house and leave temporarily, I am likely to become indignant when someone else occupies "my seat." It is funny, isn't it? Neither of these chairs is really mine. We are all borrowing heavily from the labors and efforts of others. But it takes another lens to view it this way — to see these amazing loans from the universe. Perennial wisdom has supported the idea of man as steward rather than master of our world. Traditional Native American culture emphasizes this perspective.

The improviser who experiences this principle finds security. We are not on the stage alone. We are literally surrounded by gifts and by a chain of givers who are responsible for providing them. I want you to take your place in that chain, as you see it. But you may need new eyes or a new pair of glasses to make this discovery. My realization of this truth came in rural Japan.

Looking with a New Lens

Arriving on a July morning at the Sen Kobo Temple in Kuwana, Japan, I was filled with apprehension and some excitement. High humidity and oppressive heat set the stage. The year was 1987, and I was at this Zen temple to spend a week doing an odd practice—investigating my debt to the world. I knew only that I needed to be there. I wasn't sure why, but I was listening to that inner voice, which had started speaking to me when I left Denison.

Perhaps your eye, like mine, is trained to notice certain kinds of things: what is wrong with the situation, who is a jerk, and how much others need fixing. It is so easy to find fault. Some folks are professionals at this kind of negative thinking. The practice I had come to experience, created in the early twentieth century by a Japanese businessman, Yoshimoto Ishin, promised a radically different view. Not some new age "positive thinking," the technique called Naikan offered a way to examine reality past and present from a fresh perspective.

I was there to do some bookkeeping. My task was to focus on three questions. *What had I received from others during my life? What had I given back to them? What trouble or bother had I caused them?* The questions are used to examine important relationships and are directed at key individuals in one's life. A set time frame is assigned and one moves forward chronologically. This becomes a meditation. In this formal setting you always begin reflecting on your mother (or whoever was caring for you at the time of your birth). The time periods are determined by logical groupings—earliest memories, grammar-school years, junior-high school years, etc.

For fourteen hours each day for a week, I sat quietly on a

straw mat, thinking about these three questions and using my own value system to determine what was a gift or trouble. I studied my past relationship with my mother, my father, and several important friends and mentors. I had approximately ninety minutes for each reflection period. At the end of each segment, a guide would appear, bow, and ask me to report on what I had learned. Quietly, sometimes tearfully, I spoke from the ledger of my memory, giving an account of the details that had come to light during my reflection. The guide listened silently, gave my next assignment, bowed, thanked me, and then slipped away.

What I discovered astounded me—a world that had been there, but was formerly unseen—a place where I was receiving far more than I had been giving; in short, a world of support. I walked into a brand-new movie of my life, one in which I wasn't the star, but one of many players. To see my story from the perspective of the others in my life gave it new meaning.

In order to improvise, players need to discover this less commonly known but more realistic vantage point. We need to see the contributions of others in bold relief and to recognize our interdependence. It isn't necessary to travel halfway around the world and sit in a steamy temple to learn this lesson, however. Look around.

Are you sitting right now as you read? If so, then a chair, sofa, or bed is supporting you. You probably have not paid much attention to this fact until I mentioned it. Nor have you been thinking that someone designed the chair (sofa, bed, etc.); someone manufactured it; someone brought it to where you are sitting; someone paid for it—perhaps it was you. It is likely that many people (mostly unknown to you) had a hand in the chair's creation and journey to where it is now. It is fair to say that you are receiving a service from the chair and from all of those people whose efforts were part of the story. Whether you notice it or not, whether you thank it or not, the chair offers you support, comfort. The chair is a silent gift.

Discovering Unseen Gifts

When my husband built our retirement home in 1997, he was careful to place electric outlets in many locations, generously spacing them so that we would always have access to a plug if needed. We had lived in an older apartment in San Francisco, which featured one electrical outlet per room. Ron vowed that someday we would not lack sufficient outlets. Frankly, I don't spend a lot of time contemplating wall plugs. Today was different. This morning as I lounged in bed, wrapped in my favorite green jersey-cotton sheets and patchwork quilt, enjoying a rare sleep-in on a Saturday, my attention wandered to the wall next to my bed. To my left there is a single-hung window covered by wooden venetian blinds. I close and open these blinds daily as part of my bedtime and morning rituals. Below this window and slightly to the right is a standard wall plug, a double electrical outlet. This was the very first time that I noticed the existence of this plug, even though I have been sleeping in this room for seven years. The outlet has been there all this time, patiently waiting to serve me.

I am startled by the discovery. How is it that this convenience has been in my visual field for a long time, and I have failed to see it? What else am I missing? Is there something right in front of you now waiting to offer service to you? Are there people who are giving to you, unnoticed? Perhaps they are "just doing their job" and you are the beneficiary. Who are these benefactors?

If I adopt the gift perspective, I will discover that I am in debt. Perhaps we are reluctant to look because of an unwillingness to experience this indebtedness. However, when we see ourselves as rich, in the sense of having received much, it is natural to want to give back. Understanding the debt provides a moral imperative to become a lively participant in the culture of the gift. In Lewis Hyde's anthropological study *The Gift*, he defines the nature of a gift as something that must keep on moving, and moving away from us. It is less important that we return something directly to the one who gave to us than it is that we keep the energy of the gift alive, in motion, moving forward.

The 2000 film *Pay It Forward*, starring Kevin Spacey, tells the story of a seventh-grade teacher who gave his social studies class the following assignment: "Think of an idea to change our world—and put it into action." An eleven-year-old boy comes up with a plan to do serious good deeds for three people. The beneficiaries are asked to promise to "pay it forward" by doing good deeds for three other people, and so on. The goal is to start a chain of selfless giving that moves forward.

More than twenty-five years ago I started the practice of paying for the car behind me when I cross any toll bridge. It's a way of giving something randomly on a routine basis. I learned of this from an intense, carrot-haired undergraduate named Maureen, who was a princess of generosity. She once spent weeks making a quilt that she gave to a homeless person she didn't even know. For a long time I was interested in what happened when I paid the toll. I'd look in the rearview mirror to gauge the response. Reactions to my unexpected gesture ran the gamut from elation to suspicion. One driver nearly got in an accident while rushing to catch up with me at a stop-light. He got out of his car and presented a bouquet of flowers. "Thanks," he said. "Your paying my toll was the nicest thing that's happened to me in a long time." Other drivers have sped away; fearful, I suspect, that I might want something in return. While the goal is to do something good, it isn't always received as such. I can't control how others receive a gift.

Some gifts are not objects, but support and encouragement we give each other. A recent card reminded me, "The best things in life aren't things." Often the best present you can give is encouragement and appreciation. Each of us has an unlimited bank account of credit to give away. Why not spread it around? Give the postman a special word of thanks for marching on his feet all day to bring you the mail. Give your son credit for helping with the dishes, and your spouse credit for taking out the trash or mowing the lawn. Look around at all the things others do from which you benefit. Were there cleanup crews after the big storm attending to the broken trees and downed power lines? We complain loudly if we are inconvenienced by something, but do we also speak loudly of the routine work that others are doing for us? What are they doing well? What are they doing that is difficult or thankless? Never let an hour go by without giving credit to someone.

try this:

Make a point of thanking people for thankless jobs. Look out for people doing difficult or dangerous tasks. Wave, call out, express thanks in any way that seems appropriate. Mention what you appreciate.

Giving credit seems scarce at universities. While a scholar may provide a footnote, it is rare that he makes a point of thanking others for their work. In higher education we are trained to look for what is wrong. We prize the critical life and see virtue in being able to find fault and point it out. While the critical method sharpens the mind, it dulls the heart. We fail to see what is right, what is working, what is good. Let's change this.

Look around: give thanks, give credit, give encouragement, and never stop; become liberal with your praise and acknowledgement of others, including strangers and not excluding family members. Cultivate a generosity of speech. Be extravagant with your positive findings. Watch your world grow rich as you appreciate it and speak about it often.

Understanding Interdependence

We are not alone. The improviser notices that his path has been swept by others and that many hands are making the job light. By replacing the myth of the self-made person with an understanding of our interdependence, we discover a more realistic view, especially of our relationships. It is easy to forget that we are all in this together. You may be sitting alone in a room, imagining: "Well, I'm on my own right now, aren't I, reading this book?" Yes. But you may be missing other parts of the picture. Let's do an inventory. Notice what you are receiving right now. Look around. Examine the detail.

What supports you at this moment? We began earlier in this chapter by noticing what we were sitting on. What other objects, energy sources, or people contribute to your well-being right now? Does a lamp or overhead light allow you to see this page? How did this book come to you? Who else's labor contributed to your having this book in your hand? Who gave you the money to purchase this book? You may think, "But I earned it with my labors." Yes. And another truth is that the wages were given to you by your employer. Thanks to his payroll staff and the tellers at the bank you were able to have the cash in hand to buy the book.

I write these words on a laptop computer given to me by Stanford University. The computer was purchased by a helpful department administrator named Ron who drove across town to an electronics store to pick it up. Our production manager catalogued the machine and loaded software for my use. Each of their labors makes this moment possible for me. With a little effort I can discover others whose work has contributed. What about the dockworker who loaded the cartons of computer hardware onto the trucks that brought them to the electronics store? What about Kate in the Drama office at Stanford, who processed the invoice to pay for the machine? I am in her debt, too.

The improviser knows that she is inextricably bound and dependent upon others. Everything we do (or refrain from doing) matters. My effort or my neglect of the smallest detail has consequence. The story of the butterfly on one side of the continent whose beating wings create a tidal change on the other coast makes this point. The theme of interdependence is celebrated in the television series *Joan of Arcadia*. God—who shows up in many guises, including that of the school janitor, a bratty eight-year-old, and a homeless man—speaks to Joan, a modern high-school student, and gives her simple instructions. These characters, speaking for God, advise Joan to do things—join a science club, hold a yard sale, sign up for piano lessons. At the conclusion of each episode, we discover how these seemingly random acts pay off as links to some good deed. When Joan joins the science club, she meets a boy whose father works to impound autos. One of the cars recently taken in, and now for sale, she learns, is fitted for a driver who must use hand controls. Joan's brother is disabled and needs such a vehicle. This "chance encounter" allows Joan to help her brother. It is only with hindsight that we understand these connections.

The classic film *It's a Wonderful Life,* starring Jimmy Stewart, illustrates this point. Stewart's character, distraught over a devastating business error, decides it is time to end it all, lamenting that his life wasn't worth living. At the moment when he is about to fling himself off an icy bridge, a guardian angel shows up to offer a guided tour of what the world would be like if he "had never lived." He is stunned to discover how even the smallest of his actions resulted in great benefit to others.

We may miss seeing the part that our everyday actions play in this lively web of help and support, and we often miss seeing the contributions of others. Applying the ninth maxim, we exercise a new muscle of appreciation and, as a result, grow more realistic. It is a useful lens, too, when a situation appears to be a bad one.

On Christmas Day my husband and I were en route to a holiday dinner when an inattentive driver behind us, not seeing that we had stopped to allow a car in front of us to make a turn, slammed into us. Our car was pushed into the car ahead. Being the middle of an "auto sandwich" was pretty frightening. As all of the drivers got out of their cars to point fingers, Ron and I took a deep breath and looked at what we could be grateful for. By focusing on what was right about the situation instead of what was wrong, we managed to avoid the shouting and blaming that could easily have made the situation worse. We saw the gift in the moment: that we had been spared any injury and that help was at hand.

Use this approach to create a lens for life. Train your mind to appreciate what you are receiving. Generalizations such as "I have a lot of blessings" are missing something; you need to go one more important step. Look for discrete examples of help and support. They are everywhere. The very best thank-you is one that acknowledges the detail of what you have received—thanks for *what*? I have always considered the all-purpose "thanks for everything" to be a sizable cop-out and an effortless way to appear to settle one's debt without examining it. Which of these would you rather hear: "Thanks for all you did, Aunt Gail" or "Thanks for inviting us for the holidays, and for making such a delicious pot roast and my favorite lemon tart. And I really appreciate that you invited my roommate, too. Our room was really comfortable, and we enjoyed having those soft quilts on the beds. We loved learning how to play the word game you taught us all after dinner. And please thank Uncle Claude for picking us up at the airport. His advice about graduate schools was invaluable"? It isn't always appropriate to give a full list, of course, but whenever you take the time to thank someone, go that extra step and mention something concrete.

The gifts of life come to us as separate items—a friend patiently waiting an hour outside the emergency room, the grocery worker who climbs into the warehouse to find an item that is not on the shelf, the hostess who puts fresh flowers in the guest bathroom, the teacher who remembers to bring the copy of a novel she thought you would enjoy reading, the attendant who repositions the fans in the gym to circulate the air more agreeably. Life comes to us as details. Look for them.

try this:

Make a list of what you have received from others today. Find the particulars. What unseen faces have been helping you today? Define both gifts and givers.[6]

Here are some entries from my tally today:

> *"My husband took out the trash and recycling for the weekly pickup."*
>
> *"Our insurance agent filed the accident report on our behalf."*
>
> *"The postal worker weighed my package and determined the correct postage."*
>
> *"A neighbor gave me heirloom tomatoes from her garden."*
>
> *"The road crew is resurfacing the road in front of our house."*
>
> *"My printer made copies of this draft."*
>
> *"The electric baseboard heater in this room is warming me."*

try this:

Who are your remote helpers? What person far removed from this moment (in time and/or place) has made a contribution with his work that benefits you right now? Imagine a distant contributor and trace the line of effort to the present moment.

(I have borrowed this interesting game that you can play with friends and family, perhaps when you are traveling.)[7]

For instance: The waitress who brought food to the automobile mechanic who fixed the car for the electrician that allowed him to drive to work to wire the Drama-Department building, which houses Ron, our administrator, who went to the shop to purchase the computer on which I now write this paragraph.

Can you see that each contribution is a necessary link? My present comfort is in fact the result of countless acts performed by others. Interdependence is a reality. Understanding this can provide insight as we wrestle with the question of our place in the order of things.

try this:

Practice thanksgiving. See how many times each day you can find to say thank you. Express thanks out loud, looking for variations of ways to express it ("Thanks"; "It was kind of you"; "I appreciate it"; "How thoughtful of you").

try this:

Write a thank-you note or e-mail every day. Be sure to mention the detail of what you appreciate.

[the ninth maxim]
wake up to the gifts

* Notice that the glass is half full.
* Treasure the details.
* Who or what is helping you right now?
* Make a point of thanking those with thankless jobs.
* What are you doing to give back?
* Keep the gift moving forward.
* Our smallest actions count. Everything we do has the potential to help others.
* Make "thank you" your mantra.

[the tenth maxim]
make mistakes, please

The hardest thing to learn is not "how to juggle," but how to let the balls drop.
— ANTHONY FROST, *Improvisation in Drama*

t here is a sign in my classroom that reads, "If you are not making mistakes, you are not doing improv." Mistakes are our friends, our partners in the game. They are necessary. Making mistakes is how we function. We don't consider them as something to be avoided; they are part of our operating system. The tenth maxim invites us to jump into the world of "oops" with both feet. You will have some adventures.

It may take some getting used to. Mistakes have a bad rap, and nobody likes making them. We imagine a row of stern-faced judges throwing up low scores every time we take a misstep or flounder. "Fortunately," my husband remarked, "there are no Olympic judges watching our lives." We need to start a revolution to celebrate the good that can come from seeing mistakes as natural. Public mistakes can even humanize us; someone who goes "off script" or who fumbles seems more authentic, more real—like us. Most audiences actually enjoy seeing those in the spotlight struggle and recover as long as they appear cheerful about it.

When I say, "Make mistakes, please," what I really want is for you to do something risky or challenging, something out of your comfort zone, where mistakes are possible (and likely), and to proceed boldly. Turtles are a good model, since they make progress only when they stick their necks out. We need to develop this habit. I sometimes require that my students make at least one ego-crushing mistake per class to get used to the experience. It is not the mistake that should mesmerize our attention, but rather what we do thereafter. Here is an example of how the pros handle it.

It was the New Year's Eve performance of the True Fiction Magazine improv troupe. The audience suggestion for the show's title was "Battle of the Nuns." The story progressed as Sisters Agnes, Mary, and Claire found that they were in conflict. The vicar came knocking at the door of the priory. Diane, the improviser who had been named Sister Agnes in a previous scene, answered the door. The vicar said, "I've come to see Sister Agnes." Forgetting that this was her own name, she replied, "I'll go and get her." Then, taking several steps, she recognized her mistake. "Oh, right, Sister Agnes, that's *me*," she smiled. "I guess all of us nuns look alike." The audience loved this moment.

A mistake is most often a result that we had not planned—something unexpected, an odd outcome or side journey, usually something new. Sometimes we use the word "mistake" to imply an unwanted outcome. "Coming to this movie was a mistake." While we may bemoan a blunder or miscue, the real question to ask afterward is not "How on earth did I do that?" but rather "What comes next? What can I make of this? What kind of a bonus might this be?" A constructive response to a mistake is to notice it, acknowledge it, and, if possible, use it. Artists do this all the time—

capitalize on an unplanned paint dribble. Are things not going your way? Notice the way they *are* going, and follow the situation for a while to see where you touch down. Perhaps going to that lousy movie landed you right next door to an intriguing new restaurant. Look around.

When I encourage you to make mistakes, I'm not suggesting that detail is inconsequential — far from it. The opposite is true: detail is everything. The tenth maxim is not a license for sloppy attention. If my absentmindedness results in a problem for someone, the appropriate response is an apology, of course. Don't be careless, and don't be overly careful. Our goal is resilience, and perseverance in the face of failure.

Thomas Edison's experiments to find the proper medium for the filament in the electric lightbulb produced more than 3,000 mistakes, but he learned from each failed attempt and kept on going. "Of the 200 light bulbs that didn't work, every failure told me something that I was able to incorporate into the next attempt," Edison wrote.

Of course, there are times when accuracy is essential and when a mistake does create a serious problem. Brain surgery and missile defense come to mind. However, 99.9 percent of the time, a mistake is just an unanticipated outcome giving us information. That's good.

---

try this:

Take a risk. Check out a new restaurant with cuisine that is unfamiliar to you. Order something you have never tried that seems as if it might be appealing. Expand your world of culinary experience.

Taking the Circus Bow

Matt Smith, a wonderful Seattle improv teacher and solo performer, taught me a liberating game that can be used as a response to a personal screwup. He calls it "the Circus Bow." Matt claims this is how circus clowns deal with a slip in their routines. Instead of shrinking and berating himself silently with "Oh, no, I really blew it!" the clown turns to the crowd on one side and takes a magnificent bow with his hands extended and his arms high in the air, proclaiming "Ta-dah!" as if he had just pulled off a master stunt. He then turns to face the other side of the audience and repeats the bow, "Ta-dah!" Doing it in both directions allows him a 360-degree view of where he is.

The virtue of this is that it pulls his attention out into the world again, looking around and standing tall. This engaged and forward-looking vantage point is an excellent place to be after a blooper. It is more common to focus inward when a blunder occurs. "How could I have done that?" The body shrinks and withdraws. Instead, a mistake should wake us up. Become more alert, more alive. Ta-dah! New territory. Now, what can I make of this? What comes next?

We need to let go of outcomes. This is the hard part. Naturally we have some result in mind. We want the bar mitzvah to go without a hitch. We want the carpet to be installed flawlessly, the dinner to come out of the oven like the magazine photos, the meeting to start on time, the vacation to be perfect. The more precise my vision of an outcome, the more likely I am to be disappointed. Things don't turn out as planned. You don't need to abandon your dreams; just don't let them get in the way of noticing what *is* taking place. Observe the currents of life, accept what is happening, including mistakes, and continue working to create the best outcome. The key here is a flexible mind.

Surviving a mistake can build character. In 1992 Dr. Gerhard Casper accepted the position of president of Stanford University. His inauguration in Frost Amphitheater on October 2 was a prestigious event. Dignitaries in the processional included former Stanford presidents Richard Lyman and Donald Kennedy, along with some seven thousand guests. I was invited to join the academic procession and give a dramatic reading from the writings of the university's founder, Jane Stanford. I had been called into service to portray Jane Stanford on previous occasions, but none as solemn as this.

I wore the traditional cap, gown, and academic hood under the bright California sun. The day was radiant and warm. According to the program, my reading followed a stately musical tribute to President Casper, composed for the occasion and performed by the Stanford orchestra, who were on the stage behind the academic cadre. The conductor launched the stirring piece, guiding the musicians skillfully. As the music came to an end and a small silence ensued, I rose and walked to the podium, placed my book on the stand, took a full breath, and declaimed: "And now, the words of Jane Stanford. . . ." And, at that moment the horns and violins commenced the *final movement* of the piece.

Wrong cue.

Oh, dear. I froze as I looked out at the faces of the audience. It is hard to describe my feeling at that moment. "Mortified" seems right. What I clearly needed to do was to return to my seat, enjoy (or at least, listen to) the final movement of the music, and wait for the applause. Head held high, I turned and walked back to my folding chair. I sat down and waited. The music came to a conclusion at last, and the applause followed. I rose and returned to the podium. This time as I said, "And *now,* the words of Jane Stanford," I could hear the rustle of quiet laughter and a murmur of understanding from the assembly. The truth of the moment (that I had flubbed my cue) had softened all of us. The real task for me and for the spectators was to leave the mistake behind and focus on the message I was there to deliver, Jane's dream for the future of Stanford. I rededicated myself to channeling her vision, and the reading went well. I did not let this miscue become the event, just one moment of it. When you make a mistake, turn your attention to what comes next. Focus on doing that well, with full mind and heart. Look ahead, not back.

Jim Thompson, author of *Positive Coaching,* shared the story of my Stanford inauguration gaffe with his basketball squad, along with a John Wooden quote that "the team that makes the most mistakes is going to win." Thompson encourages his athletes to play aggressively, to really go for it, and when they do make a blunder in practice to silently say "Ta-dah!" In no time at all his players were not only mumbling it under their breath, but running full tilt down the court shouting "Ta-dah!" with arms outstretched and big smiles on their faces. Thompson said he would know that they were really playing with abandon if one of them let out a "Ta-dah!" after making a mistake *during* a game.

try this:

Take a circus bow. The next time you notice that you have made a mistake, done something that feels silly or dumb, do the Circus Bow. Raise your arms in the air, smile, turn left and right. Say "Ta-dah!" brightly. Then look around and see what needs to be done next and do it. If the situation is a public one it is okay to do this silently, thinking the experience instead of speaking out loud.

Improvisers are known to collect mistakes. Encourage and allow yourself to make at least one blooper a day. Keep a tally. Congratulate yourself as you add to your mistake list. Become a confident mistake-maker. Lighten up. Notice how often a mistake can be an opportunity or even a blessing. If your mistake creates a problem for others, don't forget to apologize.

Mistakes are a natural and inevitable part of living; they will happen whether we adopt the way of the planner or the way of the improviser. This story of two cooks, a true fable, makes this point.

Cooking: Two Ways

Our national cooking maven, the beloved Julia Child, who died in the summer of 2004, was remembered as often for her flexibility and good humor as for her culinary prowess. Her naturalness around kitchen disasters encouraged generations of cooks. Francis X. Clines, writing in the *New York Times*, eulogized: "Mistakes were not the end of the world, just part of the game. In fact minor slips and mishaps were weekly events of 'The French Chef,' and none of them seemed to faze Mrs. Child."

Cooking is an ideal paradigm for viewing the question of mistake-making. Two of my friends approach the task differently. Celia and Dalla both love to cook. Each enjoys the pleasure of eating well and sharing food with friends and family. Those eating at their table often say (of both cooks): "You should open a restaurant!" They have contrasting styles — one is a planner, one is an improviser.

Celia subscribes to all the gourmet magazines and reads them cover to cover. She takes cooking classes and pores over cookbooks, devouring them like novels. She visits the local farmers' markets weekly and surfs Internet sites for exotic ingredients and specialty foods. Celia plans carefully and arrives at a perfect menu, sometimes spending days driving around town to specialty shops and greengrocers to gather ingredients. On cooking days she follows the recipes carefully. Indeed, her meals are sometimes works of art. Many of them are delicious, some are so-so, and a few are, shall we say, not so great . . . but all do feed her guests. Celia hates making mistakes, but they do happen even when she follows a recipe faithfully.

Dalla occasionally reads cookbooks and food articles, but not very often. She does spend a lot of time in her vegetable garden, however. Her basic cooking strategy is to look around at what is closest to her. First, she opens the refrigerator to see what "needs to be eaten." Then she examines her garden to see what is ready to be harvested.

She is a wizard at using up what she calls "twiddledee-bits" (small amounts of leftovers, sauces, liquids, etc., including a teaspoon of fading brown mustard in a jar that most people would have simply thrown out). Dalla can't bear to see any food go to waste, so her central cooking approach is to take what is already there and compose it in such a way that it is delicious, or at least palatable. She has a way of blending foods and seasoning them so that the original leftovers are no longer recognizable—a new dish is created. Leftover stir-fry turns into soup, leftover soup gets folded into spaghetti sauce, and leftover spaghetti sauce is used for pizza topping. I asked her once about a curried vegetable soup that I had found extraordinary. What on earth was her secret ingredient? She replied: "Perhaps it's the tablespoon of jalapeño jelly that I was trying to get rid of. Someone had kindly given me this strange jelly, and I finally used the last of it in this soup!" Surely no recipe on earth includes adding jalapeño jelly to a vegetable soup. Dalla isn't afraid of trying something and making a mistake. From the perspective of taste many of the meals are delicious, some are so-so, and a few are, shall we say, not so great . . . but all do feed her guests.

Notice that both cooks—Celia, the planner, and Dalla, the improviser—have about the same number of successes and failures. Both make mistakes. Planning carefully is no guarantee that things will turn out error-free. And improvising is not a magic pill for success.

There is even a melodious French word that describes Dalla's method: *bricolage*. It's the art of commandeering the materials at hand—what is most obvious—to solve the problem. This way of doing things turns limitations into assets. You start by carefully noticing what is available. It is a mind-set—a deeply ecological approach. Improvising, or dealing artfully with what is already there, can be understood not only as a backup approach, but also as a way of life.

try this:

Experiment with the principle of bricolage.
Instead of running to the store to buy something, solve
a problem using only the materials at hand. For example,
use the comics or an old calendar as gift wrap. Create a
meal with what you already have.

Admitting Mistakes

Realists understand the wisdom of the tenth maxim. Great
undertakings routinely involve risk; trying something new
may bring unwanted results. We all know that it is possible to
bungle even an ordinary or familiar task. While most bloopers
don't require a mea culpa, some mistakes do. When things
that involve trust go wrong, speak up right away. It just makes
sense to do so. Knowing that mistakes are inevitable, and admitting them freely, demonstrates courage and character.

In interviews for *The Fog of War,* Robert McNamara confessed that if they were honest, all high-ranking military
officials (including him) would have to admit that they had
made mistakes that had resulted in needless deaths during
wartime. We never hear this, of course. Inevitably denial is
the reply to any public accusation. However, disavowing a
mistake rarely fools anyone. Officials who bend over back-
ward rather than admit an error appear shortsighted and
cartoonlike. Wouldn't it be wiser to cultivate honesty? Join
me in the campaign to "fess up when we really mess up"!

[the tenth maxim]
make mistakes, please

* If you are not making mistakes, you are not improvising.
* Be like a turtle: stick out your neck to make progress.
* When you screw up, say "Ta-dah!" and take a bow.
* Mistake? Focus on what comes next.
* Let go of outcomes. Cultivate a flexible mind.
* Mistakes may actually be blessings.
* Become a confident mistake-maker. Lighten up.
* Try bricolage—use what is there artfully.
* Admitting a mistake shows character.

[the eleventh maxim]
act now

I cannot do
All the good
That the world
Needs
But the world
Needs all the good
That I can do.

— JANA STANFIELD,
"All the Good," *Let the Change Begin*

t he essence of improvisation is action — doing it in real time. We act in order to *discover* what comes next. We act because we have a purpose or a question. Using action as our first response is not always easy, however. For many of us moving forward comes only after reflection, comparison, and planning; we think we must *decide* on our course. Only when we are sure, when we've got, as my grandmother used to say, "all of our ducks in a row," do we proceed.

The eleventh maxim reminds us of the power of action as part of the discovery process. For the improviser it is: ready, *fire,* aim. We begin before there is a plan. What we do moves us forward and gives us more information about how to proceed. The doing itself becomes the teacher and guide. Nike's snappy logo "Just do it" reminds us that it's unnecessary to be motivated, get ourselves together, or even feel like doing it. The key is to get up and go. "For all my dreams, I am what I do," muses psychologist David K. Reynolds. We know this, but taking action may appear daunting.

Sometimes it seems as if there are hurdles that must first be overcome. Suppose your obstacle has a fancy name like "writer's block." Conventional wisdom suggests that this needs attention. Adam, a television writer struggling with this, lamented, "I wish I could figure out why I keep putting off the work I need to do. It makes me miserable." He went to a counselor and discussed it every week. He speculated that if he could find the cause of his resistance he would get back to writing.

As I saw the problem, insight wasn't the answer. Even if he had that great *aha!* he would still need to show up at his desk and turn on the computer. Natalie Goldberg's first rule for writers, "Keep your hand moving," was the best advice for him.

Any worthwhile job has its share of tasks that aren't easy or appealing. Putting off those we like least provides a double penalty: the work looms and we consider ourselves failures. Scheduling the dreaded jobs and sticking to our schedule can help. So if you can't get out of it, *get into it*

try this:

Schedule that job you have been avoiding. Write it on your calendar or in your date book. Set a specific time and show up. Focus on taking the first step. What action will begin the task? (Making a phone call? Pulling everything out of the refrigerator? Assembling papers? Picking up the broom? Writing an apology note?)

A Japanese psychiatrist, Dr. Shōma Morita (a contemporary of Sigmund Freud), founded a mental-health movement—Morita Therapy—based on the healing power of action. He helped his patients to see that constructive action was already a cure, suggesting that instead of trying to overcome their neurotic thinking, they should focus on doing what they needed to do in their lives and doing it well.

Improvisers understand Dr. Morita's insistence on the eminence of behavior. On the improv stage action creates the world of play. There are no huddles in the back room. Motivation is not required. Good intentions, beliefs, resolutions, even promises don't matter. Action does.

I watched a woman sitting in her car in our local shopping center buckle her seat belt, open her car door, and toss a used beverage cup under the car. She slammed the driver's door and drove away, leaving the paper cup lying on the cement, half filled with liquid, dribbling, the straw poking out of the lid. My first thought was: "Why do people care so little about our environment?" And, almost before the judgment had formed fully, I walked over to the empty parking space, picked up the cup, and disposed of it in a nearby receptacle. When I see something that needs to be done, I usually do it without debate. The improviser in me is trained to take action rather than muse over whose job it may be. It is always my job if I see it to do, and I'm able to do the task.

And it is a wise idea to tackle important tasks early. Procrastinating with an essential job compounds the problem. The specter of it haunts. Start your day by doing what is vital to your well-being. A celebrated anthropologist confided that he always does the hard thing first in the very early morning hours. For him that meant writing. What is most important to you?

---

try this:

Do the essential job first. What is it that really *needs* to be done? Try doing it first thing in the morning.

Acting with a Buddy

Acting can be easier when you have company. Joining a class or a club is a natural way to increase your chances to get going. Improvising is a collaborative art, and when members of a group show up, action naturally follows. We get energy from one another. What seems like a chore when alone can become a party when done with a gang of friends. Sharing work is a time-honored strategy—think of the quilting bee or a barn raising. Are there modern equivalents in your life?

And don't overlook the power of the buddy system. Are your friendships based solely on supportive talk? Why not strengthen the bonds through action? Relationships grow when we do useful things together. Be the instigator.

---

try this:

Harness the power of friendship. Make plans with a friend to meet regularly for something you both need to do. (Show up three times a week at 7:00 in the morning for a power walk, for example.) Or invite a buddy to join you in a job you have been putting off. (Clean out your closet together, selecting clothes to give to charity.) Make a pact to trade help and join your friend in doing something.

Not Doing: Scorpions on the Path

You might think the rule "act now" is a prescription for work mania. It is not. Constructive action arises from clear purposes. (Remember the eighth maxim: stay on course.) Sometimes what is needed is inaction—waiting, resting. Charging ahead can be foolhardy. An improv saying that reminds us of this is: "Don't just do something. Stand there." Our goal is always *appropriate* action, doing what is needed. Occasionally this means doing nothing while being watchful or waiting for others to act before proceeding.

As an improviser I am in training to keep the whole picture in perspective. A reflexive reaction to a situation can rob me of a truly intelligent response. Everyone has blind spots. Checking to see if my initial reaction is appropriate is wise.

On a morning walk through Stern Grove in San Francisco, I passed a strange animal. It was about nine inches long, maroon in color, and it looked like a small lobster or crawfish. Only it wasn't in or by the lake; it was right in the middle of the cement walkway, far from any water. The creature, which I later determined to be a rather large scorpion, was very much alive and moving in an easterly direction, the same way that I was going. He was progressing slowly. I paused to inspect him as he crawled forward, lobster-style. Apparently his senses had not yet detected me coming from behind.

Twenty minutes later on the return walk, I encountered him again; this time I was moving straight toward him. As I entered his field of vision (or sense) the little fellow lurched into an abrupt attack position, standing on his hind legs, waving his scary pincers at me. He was executing a two-legged war dance, probably a defense strategy. "Fair enough," I thought. "Nature at work." I continued on my way, and ten yards later I looked back to see that he was still on his hind legs, menacing the air. Although the threat had clearly passed, he was still defending himself. Poor fellow, he was wasting so much energy. He had failed to notice that the big shadow was far away now and had never shown any signs of harming him.

The incident made me think about first reactions and how common it is to substitute a habitual response for a considered one. We've all experienced a knee-jerk reaction. Notice that reactions have two parts: how I feel and what I do. As I clean off the desk, I find a two-months-overdue telephone bill. (My husband is ordinarily responsible, and unpaid bills are red flags to me.) Initially, I focus on my emotions. I'm upset. If I act on the feeling alone I may well speak to my husband in an accusing manner. Instead, if I consider what needs to be done, I can approach the situation more constructively. First I need to find out if, indeed, the bill *is* still overdue. It's possible that it has been paid. If it hasn't, I need to figure out what I can do to remedy the situation. Perhaps this is the opportunity for what David K. Reynolds calls a "secret service," to pay the bill myself, although it probably wouldn't remain secret in the long run.

With only a moment's reflection, I discover that I don't need to wave my arms at all. It is a poor habit to allow emotions to dictate behavior. No feeling is ever a justification for strident words or a discourteous act. While I cannot control my first reaction to an event, I can control what I do thereafter. Choose your behavior mindfully. That's real personal power.

Doing It a Different Way

The call to action ("act now") provides a platform for developing flexibility. In the third maxim: just show up, we discussed the value of changing *where* we are. With the eleventh maxim you can discover the unexpected benefits that come from changing *how* you do something. Try doing it a different way.

---

try this:

Change some simple habit. For example, instead of using a mug, experiment by drinking your morning coffee from a bowl, the way the French do, or from a small glass, as people do in Turkey. Instead of walking briskly from your car to the office, try a different pace—walk very slowly, observing everything.

---

try this:

Change your daily schedule by one hour and see what happens. Start by going to bed an hour earlier than you normally do. The next day, get up an hour earlier and leave for work an hour earlier. When you get to work, do something you haven't done before:

take a walk, read a magazine, clean off your desk, just breathe and enjoy the extra time. Do your work on schedule and then go home. Remember to go to bed an hour earlier than normal. If there's a TV program that you normally watch, tape it, if you can, so that you can watch it at a more convenient time.

try this:

Go home a new way. Find another route from your home to work (or from your apartment to the store) and take the new path. Pay attention to the landmarks and the vegetation. Become a traveler in your own neighborhood. You may wish to take a different route every day for a week and see what you find.

[the eleventh maxim]
act now

* The essence of improvising is action.
* Act in order to discover what comes next.
* You don't need to feel like doing something to do it.
* Schedule a difficult task and stick to your timetable.
* Invite a buddy to join you in doing what you need to do.
* Do the hard thing first.
* To find a new perspective, try doing something a different way.
* Sometimes *not doing* is what is needed.
* If you can't get out of it, *get into it.*

[the twelfth maxim]
take care of each other

We are creatures of community. Those individuals, societies, and cultures who learned to take care of each other, to love each other, and to nurture relationships with each other during the past several hundred thousand years were more likely to survive than those who did not.

— DR. DEAN ORNISH, "Love and Survival"[8]

imagine a small boat on the high sea. In it are five improvisers, all hoping to weather the storm. These players know that they need one another's attention and help for survival. The actor's nightmare is being in front of a paying audience without a script. So how do they do it? Each one works for the welfare of the others. Selfishness can have no part in this. While a player who is out for herself may succeed as a stand-up comic, she won't make it as part of a good improv ensemble. Consummate improvisers are marked by their generosity, courtesy, and ability to watch out for the needs of their teammates. A person who observes the twelfth maxim is someone you would want with you in a foxhole.

We are told early in training to make our partner look good, to do whatever is necessary to honor and advance all of his offers. The safety, welfare, and reputation of each player are in the hands of his team members. In practical terms we agree to take care of each other.

There's a Zen koan about two monks walking along an embankment in the dead of winter. A blizzard rages, and the snow is deep. The elder monk slips off the narrow path and falls ten feet into a snowy crevasse. The younger monk assesses the circumstance and sees that there is no way to pull his friend to safety. The koan asks what the young monk should do. The answer to this puzzle is that the young monk should jump into the abyss with his fellow monk. Sometimes the only thing we can do is to join the suffering of others—to be there alongside them. There is no fix, no remedy. But we dare not leave our comrade alone in distress.

Improvisers are quick to join a player who appears to be struggling on stage. Where possible, they do something to improve the situation. When this is out of the question, like for the young monk in the story, they are simply there, alongside their flailing friend.

We know that some suffering is inevitable and cannot be fixed. Loved ones fall seriously ill. Accidents happen. Pets die. Tragedy strikes. At these times our capacity to help and care for one another is tested. The improv stage can be seen as a permanent crisis zone where players give their best to one another, make sacrifices, fall down together, pull one another up, and if all else fails, jump into the abyss as a fellow sufferer.

Once members of a group have experienced the exhilaration and security that comes from this level of support, they recognize that it is the heart of working together. It is like having a guardian angel (or group of them) taking care of you all the time. Plus, if you adopt the twelfth maxim you are in training to *be* a guardian angel.

try this:

Become a guardian angel. Pick a friend, coworker, or family member and decide to look out for this person. Maintain a watchful eye to see if there is anything you can do to smooth his path, make her world brighter, or help him with his projects. Write her notes of thanks or encouragement.

Sharing Control

On the improv stage players work together seamlessly, in a manner that can appear mystical to outsiders. Observers often suspect that skillful improvisers are actually executing some formula or preplan: it seems impossible that human beings can cooperate so harmoniously without some prior agreement. Stephen Nachmanovitch describes the phenomenon in *Free Play*.

> I play with my partner; we listen to each other; we mirror each other; we connect with what we hear. He doesn't know where I'm going, I don't know where he's going, yet we anticipate, sense, lead, and follow each other. There is no agreed-on structure or measure, but once we have played for five seconds there is a structure, because we've started something. We open each other's minds like an infinite series of Chinese boxes. A mysterious kind of information flows back and forth, quicker than any signal we might give by sight or sound. The work comes from neither one artist nor the other, even though our

own idiosyncrasies and styles, the symptoms of our original natures, still exert their natural pull. Nor does the work come from a compromise or halfway point (averages are always boring!), but from a third place that isn't necessarily like what either one of us would do individually. What comes is a revelation to both of us. There is a third, a totally new style that pulls on us. It is as though we have become a group organism that has its own nature and its own way of being, from a unique and unpredictable place which is the group personality or group brain.[9]

Learning how to work together moment by moment without a known formula is the essence of improvisation. We recognize this ability when we watch jazz musicians, giving and taking stage, harmonizing, creating a piece of music before us, and finding an ending just when it is needed. This wordless synchronicity can be found in ordinary life as well. Great teams have it. They watch each other carefully and seem to know just when to act and when to hang back. I've seen a restaurant kitchen that flows with this kind of communication. Zen monastery kitchens are sometimes like this. Perhaps you've been part of a team, ensemble, choir, musical group, or committee that worked in this way. Clearly, the ideal of teamwork is what fuels countless workshops, seminars, and wilderness experiences. It's possible to train ordinary people to work like improvisers. The improv "talent," which involves listening carefully, observing the actions of others, contributing, supporting, leading, following, filling in the gaps, and looking for the appropriate ending, can be taught and learned.

For those of us who value independence, sharing control can be the hardest lesson of all. My students know a lot about either leading or following. From the improvisers' perspective there are drawbacks to the traditional way of handling control. While it may be easy for a leader to take charge, make all the decisions, and run the show, his vision alone feeds the process. His "followers" are simply along for the ride to carry out instructions. A successful follower must subordinate his ideas and preferences to the will of the leader. The follower has the payoff of being rewarded for obedience and not rocking the boat. The leader, of course, must generate all the ideas and give instructions to everyone.

In the improv world the working paradigm is one of shared control. It differs from the "I lead and you follow" model in that both parties must stay alert and energized and actual leadership is likely to change moment by moment. Both (or all, if more than two) are always responsible, while neither (or no one) is "in control" in an absolute sense. The rule is that all improvisers have the right and responsibility to move the scene forward, adjusting always to what the new reality is. Doing what needs to be done becomes the guiding principle.

When this principle is working optimally, players report that it feels as if no one is actually in charge, but rather that all are surrendering to the story that is carrying them forward. It's more like a Ouija board working well: neither participant is pushing the pointer, but both are receiving the message. The skill that the improviser cultivates here is attention to the needs of the moment and an outward focus. She becomes the bystander who knows that what needs to be done is to pull the passenger out of the wrecked car or to provide a villain if things are going too well in a story. With shared control you must constantly wake up to the moment and act on that information.

The old response "It's not my job" is never an acceptable excuse for the improviser. It's always my job, if the job needs doing and I am there to do it. It's the difference between the following two strategies for keeping the kitchen clean: in the "Left Brain House" all the jobs are carefully assigned and posted on the house bulletin board. Mary washes dishes on Friday. Tom cooks. Celeste empties garbage. Therefore, if Celeste enters the kitchen and observes a pile of dirty dishes staring at her, she can with impunity walk right past them and grab the garbage bag. When she has finished dumping the bag, she can sit with her feet up and watch TV, while gloating that her work is "done" and Mary's isn't. In the "Right Brain House" (of improvisers) all three of our players are responsible for whatever needs doing. Using this model, whoever sees the dishes first will wash them. If, over time, one player notices that the work is not really being shared, then perhaps a reminder to other members of the team would be sufficient to right this. Those who "drive" (always control or dominate the situation) and those who "wimp" (fail to contribute or accept responsibility) are making improv errors. Pointing this out to the player would be enough to begin a correction. The improvisers' spirit is fiercely egalitarian.

I believe that human beings want to cooperate with one another but old patterns and reflexes keep them from the discovery of the delight of the give-and-take that comes from shared control. My husband and I use this model of working together on many household chores. Sharing control has many lessons, among them the value of staying alert while remaining silent and/or doing nothing. We are always responsible, but never in true control of the situation. And it is essential that we play our part. Isn't this just like life?

tips for sharing control

Become really alert. Open your eyes.

Breathe and remind yourself to relax.

Notice what's going on—attention, attention, attention.

Watch what others are doing and saying.

When you see something that needs to be done, do it.

Keep adjusting to how *it is* rather than how you'd *like it to be*.

Make your partner look good—support him or her.

Make sense out of the moment.

Notice mistakes as they occur, then refocus on what's needed to continue.

Keep on acting, even while wondering if it's the right thing to do.

Playing with Kindness

Of all accolades given my group, the Stanford Improvisors, the one of which I am most proud is: "SImps are the nicest players in the league. They are just so darned pleasant to be around." Not all groups emphasize courtesy as an essential element of their play, but we do. Working together with so many unknowns, sometimes kindness among players is all we have. Certainly it is one of the ways that we care for each other. So often, the opposite message, "Take care of yourself," is the one that is reinforced.

In an effort to understand how we perceive our world, environmental journalist Bill McKibben did an unusual experiment. In 1990 he had a Fairfax, Virginia, cable company tape their entire channel lineup of programs for a twenty-four-hour period. Then he took the 1,700 hours' worth of videotape home with him to the Adirondacks for a year and watched it. His findings, which are chronicled in the book *The Age of Missing Information,* should not come as a surprise. In a speech he gave in Vermont, he summarized:

> It's not just that there's so much chatter and clutter constantly coming at us. There's a very deep message coming at us through that chatter — a signal through all that noise. When I thought about all that TV that I watched, the residual idea, the central theme, is that each of us is the center of the universe — the most important thing on earth. We're being told we're the heaviest object around and that everything needs to orbit around our ideas of convenience and comfort — this Bud's for you.[10]

He went on to say that although this message appeals to some part of our nature, at a deeper level we know better. "It's clear that we evolved to be in more contact with the natural world than we now are, to move our muscles and our senses, to interact with all of the life that evolved alongside us. And we evolved to be in contact with each other, not just by email, but flesh to flesh, face to face, in community."[11] This is one of the great appeals of improvising together.

Playing with consideration and kindness promotes a sense of security. This is necessary when we are doing crazy, risky things—it is essential during chaos. Competition is replaced by cooperation. These old-fashioned virtues must be unearthed, studied, and practiced. It should be obvious that these values transcend the improv stage. Kindness pays off with coworkers, friends, and neighbors. And a good family requires it. Consider the convenience of others. Give up criticizing. Listen attentively. Pay attention to your partner's story. Look for ways that you can advance his dreams and interests.

My husband, Ron, is a marathon runner. I'm a couch potato basically, and at heart I am not much interested in sports. He comes alive when he describes his runs, complete with details of the water stops and the variations in his heart rate. For years I have pretended to listen until I could change the subject back to something that interested me. Recently, however, I've begun listening to his tales of running, and I ask questions about his experience. To friends I praise his efforts and goals. I bought him a subscription to a runners' magazine, and I accompany him on his trips to out-of-town races. I volunteered to give out sports drinks at the Silicon Valley marathon. I'm now on the lookout for things that I can do to support his love of running.

It should come as no surprise that my attitude shift produced a positive result: I became interested in his world, and I no longer need to fake my attention. While I haven't yet signed up for the Boston marathon, I did join a women's gym, and I am having fun training. Now Ron and I trade stories about our workouts. Looking for ways to "make my partner look good" started this chain of happy events. It has made our love grow. Kindness has a way of returning tenfold to the giver.

You cannot improvise successfully without applying the rule of consideration. Adding it to one's life can deepen relationships and cultivate friendship, and it can even mend a marriage. Doing things in a kindly way and also doing kind things—both are important.

In 1947 David Dunn, a business counselor and banker, wrote an article that first appeared in *Forbes* and later in *Reader's Digest*. It was published finally as a small book entitled *Try Giving Yourself Away*. Dunn describes an experiment in which he did just this every day. Each of us has different things to give, he points out, and what we see as a gift is an individual matter. "Some of us have spare time; others have surplus mental or physical energy; others have a special art, skill, or talent; still others have ideas, imagination, the ability to organize, the gift of leadership."[12] Once committed to this goal, Dunn discovered countless small acts that he could do to accomplish it.

A principle he followed was to give voice to any positive thought he had. If he was sitting in a restaurant and enjoying a delicious dish, he would always let someone know. He might walk directly into the kitchen and compliment the cook, or, on arriving home, write a note. He often did research to find out who was responsible for something he liked, and then contacted them with praise and appreciation.

Recently I wrote a letter of thanks to the CEO of Google, the Internet search engine that started its life at Stanford. It occurred to me that this free product was making my life easier in dozens of ways. I cited twenty examples of how the product had helped me in that week alone—finding a photo of the nursing home in Virginia where my father had been taken, booking a room at a bed-and-breakfast in Vienna for a Christmas trip, converting square footage to cubic measure, buying airline tickets, checking on the location of a local restaurant, researching a quotation, locating an old friend. A few weeks later, a package for me arrived from the company, which included a complimentary T-shirt, baseball cap, pen, and blank book. No matter how I try to give back, it seems the world keeps on giving to me.

try this:

Consider others first. Devote a whole day to putting the convenience of others ahead of your own. Check this against your habitual response. Notice when this is hard for you. Discover how rich this can make you feel.

try this:

Do something kind for the planet. Remember the "Random Acts of Kindness" bumper sticker? Look around for a small thing that needs to be done in your neighborhood or work environment. Without taking credit or telling anyone, do something nice. (Pick up debris that missed the trash can; water a plant that appears neglected; or move a fallen branch across a trail, for example.)

Really Listening: Kindness in Action

Listen with all you've got. Improvisers must be the world's best listeners, since every word spoken is vital. Listening is raised to the level of art among professionals. Players will need to remember facts mentioned only once. The most seemingly insignificant detail can become the focus of the story, so everything said (or done, for that matter) must be understood and remembered.

Actors in the True Fiction Magazine group do a simple exercise. One person speaks for three minutes, telling a story or describing something with a lot of fine points. Her partner listens intently. When the storyteller finishes, the listening partner immediately begins to repeat the story, verbatim if possible. The goal is to reproduce the speaker's words exactly. The challenge is to retain details and place names in the order spoken. This may seem a daunting task, but with a little practice, it is possible. We can all become better at this. A little effort is required, but the results can be amazing. W. A. Mathieu's wonderful resource, aptly titled *The Listening Book,* provides a treasury of simple games and exercises for those who want to be better listeners.

---

try this:

Listen as if your life depended upon it. Listen not only for content but also for tone and rhythm, for the quality of what is being said. Challenge yourself to remember what you hear.

Being Generous

Generosity is a corollary to kindness. A generous person is a wealthy one. It has nothing to do with how much we have and everything to do with our willingness to give or share.

Generosity is related to the "yes and" rule. Players know that part of their contract is to give more than is asked.

At Stanford I was invited several times to give a team-building workshop for lively groups of young entrepreneurs who had been chosen to participate in the elite Mayfield Fellows Program (MFP), a nine-month work/study curriculum designed to develop a theoretical and practical understanding of the techniques needed to grow emerging technology companies. Professor Tom Byers, director of the program, shared the group's guiding principles. These five rules are essential for the successful entrepreneur, he told me:

1. Show up on time.
2. Be nice to people.
3. Do what you say you'll do.
4. Deliver more than you promise.
5. Work with enthusiasm and passion.

These rules sound a lot like improv advice. The reminder that an entrepreneur should always deliver *more* than she promises is a great rule for life. Whenever possible, be generous.

As we cultivate the habit of taking care of one another it is natural to extend that respectful way of working to the environment and to the things of our life. Caring for objects that serve us makes perfect sense; respect need not stop with people. In his delightful book of recipes and spiritual reflections *Tomato Blessings and Radish Teachings,* Edward Espe Brown gives us a prescription that comes from a Zen saying: "Use two hands to carry one thing instead of one hand to carry two things."[13]

[the twelfth maxim]
take care of each other

* Be someone's guardian angel. Make your partner look good.
* Rescue or join someone struggling.
* Share control; don't hog it.
* Kindness is essential during chaos or a crisis.
* Try giving yourself away.
* Always put positive thoughts into words and action.
* Do "random acts of kindness."
* Put other people's convenience ahead of your own.
* Listen as if your life depended on it.
* Deliver more than you promise.

[the thirteenth maxim]
enjoy the ride

Sometimes your joy is the source of your smile, but
sometimes your smile can be the source of your joy.
— THICH NHAT HANH

i'm sorry for the disturbance that our rowdiness causes, but I've never found a way to teach improv that isn't boisterous. My classroom in the Drama Department at Stanford rings with noise, thumping, shrieks, and gales of laughter. Passersby wonder how this levity can contribute to serious learning. It does. Having fun loosens the mind. A flexible mind works differently from a rigid mind. The pleasure that accompanies our mirth makes learning easier and creates a climate for social as well as intellectual discovery. Of course, laughter isn't a prerequisite, but there is no need to exclude it from the learning process.

So, if you can, have fun. Enjoy your life. Both the Buddha and the Mona Lisa have a shy smile on their faces. Perhaps, even amid suffering there is something to grin about. Traditionally, "fun" isn't a word associated with work or getting the job done. It happens after work. Children and puppies have fun. Adults engage in serious work: "enjoyment" isn't part of that lexicon. Let's change all that.

I am inspired by the creativity of a former student who is using the sunshine of humor to teach what is often dry subject matter—nutrition. Dr. Bradley Nieder wrote to me recently to share his story after leaving Stanford. Calling himself "the Healthy Humorist," Brad is a full-time physician who is also a successful public speaker. He promotes healthful living (eating well, exercising, etc.) with jokes, rhymes, and funny stories, using the improv skills he learned in class. In reply to a query about laughter being the best medicine, he confessed, "After all, penicillin is a better medicine. And morphine works wonders, too. But laughter is still very powerful."[14]

Science recognizes the value of play in nature. Animals galumph, rolling in leaves, working off excess energy and calories, playing. My aging cat passes hours chasing and batting a paper ball made from a wadded toilet-paper wrapper—pure play. Enjoyment is a way of approaching an activity, not the activity itself. I have a friend who can turn a trip to Disneyland into work with her obsessive need to see and do everything in an orderly fashion. On the other hand, cleaning out the attic or garage can be a playful activity, if you turn on your favorite upbeat music and dance your way into cobwebs, stopping to take pleasure in the odd treasures lurking there.

Enjoy the ride, if you can. The aging bumper-sticker saying "Angels fly because they take themselves lightly" reminds us of the benefits of finding perspective. Step back, take a breath, and lighten up. The instruction "enjoy life" is an easy sell. Everybody wants to be happy and to avoid suffering. The trick, of course, is to learn how to have fun. What constitutes enjoyment? How can we bring it home?

Nearly everyone who joins the improv world as spectator or participant cites "because it is a lot of fun" as a reason for their involvement. Those who would avoid "Improving

Your Communication with Others" as too dull will flock to "Improvisation Games—Laugh Your Way to Better Relationships." There is something about playing games, making up stories, and performing zany challenges that appeals to the kid in all of us, that reminds us of times when life was simpler.

At Stanford, where learning is very *serious,* improv is a welcome relief. We need to be reminded of our capacity for delight and pleasure. Finding wonder, remembering how to play, inhabiting a classroom where there are no wrong answers— these are things we all yearn for. If we lose touch with our faculty for play, we do so at our peril. We all know people who look for this joy in all the wrong places—by trying to get high on whatever turns them on—drugs, shopping, winning. . . .

It takes so little to create the context for human play. First, we must be in the same room physically so that we can touch each other. It is useful to have a few rules to follow (or break) and a willingness to make mistakes together. Having a guide or teacher helps, but isn't necessary. What creates natural laughter? The unexpected, the spontaneous, giving without thought of return, falling down and getting up, being playful, being silly—these things can bring joy. Create a space where there are no wrong answers. Hang out there. Invite some friends. Improvise.

---

try this:

Make up the words to a song right now and sing it. You can invent the tune or go ahead and use a melody that you already know—just add new words. Sing about your day. Now.

♫ ♫ ♫ ♫ ♩♩♩♩ ♫ ♫ ♫

One graduation weekend the seniors in my group produced a graduation improv show for parents and friends. They played together one last time, performing challenges (a scene in Shakespearean verse about their chemistry final . . .). I watched the faces of the audience enjoying the mayhem—they had smiles as big as Texas, and I was reminded that it takes so little to produce a lot of pleasure: the human presence, playing together, making mistakes, solving riddles and problems, laughing, getting it right, getting it wrong, singing a song.

---

try this:

Play games together. Invite friends over for a "gaming night" and potluck. Try this easy game: How Many Uses for This Object? Pick a simple household object (a wooden spatula, a casserole lid, a dish towel, etc.) and pass it around the group. As each person holds the object, he suggests a possible use until no one can think of anything. (Holding the spatula up like a microphone, I might say, "It's a mike!" Ron mimes paddling: "It's a canoe paddle.") The last person with an idea wins. Note that there are no wrong answers. Make up your own games, or gear up for the classic Charades. When was the last time you played Twenty Questions? (Is it animal, vegetable, or mineral?)

Smiling

While waiting for a mechanic to repair a flat tire, I entered a small sandwich shop. My interaction with the lone waitress behind the counter was memorable. She was in her early sixties, with graying hair pulled back into a bun, and she was wearing the widest and most sincere smile that I had seen in some time. She looked me straight in the eye, appearing genuinely pleased to be serving me. I was struck by the quality of her attention. I ordered a tuna-fish sandwich on whole wheat. "Would you like that toasted? It'll only take a minute. And how about a free pickle?" she said, beaming. I accepted both offers and watched as she carefully prepared the sandwich. She smiled broadly again as she delivered my order, assuring me that she was eager to provide anything else I might want. Here was a worker doing a simple job who was fully engaged, who showed all the signs that she was enjoying her work, her life. Why is this a rare thing?

I sometimes hear complaints from adult students that their jobs aren't creative or rewarding. I wonder. Joy seems not so much dependent on the conditions of our external reality as it is on our way of looking at life. We apportion value. It is not intrinsic. The waitress was finding joy in her work, making sandwiches and serving them to guests. She did not demand that the job "be joyful."

Beyond all other freedoms our greatest liberty is our ability to choose our attitude. Viktor Frankl documented this great truth in his moving book *Man's Search for Meaning*. I tell improvisers to offer a pleasing face to the group. Look at one another with encouraging eyes. Avoid a scowl or judgmental look. Be a good actor. Make someone else's day. Travel guru Rick Steves has a formula for the right way to approach travel. "Be fanatically positive and militantly optimistic. If something's not to your liking, change your liking."[15]

try this:

Spend one whole day giving away smiles to everyone you encounter. Smile at yourself in the mirror, too. Notice the effect of a smile.

Fun isn't always possible, of course, and it is never a prerequisite for doing what we need to do. Some jobs require persistence and action, whether they are appealing or not. Never give up on something simply because it doesn't seem enjoyable. Wishing it were so is unrealistic. The point of the thirteenth maxim is to look for ways to enjoy what we are doing instead of waiting until we are engaged in a pleasurable task.

I really like washing dishes. I focus on the feeling of the warm water, the soapy bubbles, and the service I've received from the different items in the sink. I often slow down, savoring the experience—but not always. Sometimes I just wash dishes, fun or no.

try this:

Schedule an event that is all about fun. Do it for a friend, or better still, with someone who needs cheering up (perhaps a senior or a child in a hospital): making balloon animals, a hayride, skinny-dipping in a pool, a karaoke party, break-dancing lessons, attending an improv show, touring an ice-cream factory. Have fun. Enjoy your life. Seriously.

[the thirteenth maxim]
enjoy the ride

* Find joy in whatever you are doing, including ordinary tasks.
* Look for ways to play. Play is essential to human growth.
* Learning is enhanced when we lighten up.
* Laughter is good medicine.
* If something is not to your liking, change your liking.
* Give away smiles every day.
* Do something just for the fun of it.

[epilogue]

Some improvisations take longer than others. It will seem comically ironic that a little book on the subject of improvising has taken me more than twenty years to write. The first draft of this manuscript dates back to 1981. I have, in addition to dozens of three-ring binders gathering dust on my shelves, a bewildering array of backup disks—the old five-and-a-quarter-inch floppy kind, the more modern three-and-a-half-inch plastic disks, 100M Zip-drive disks, and, more recently, what are called USB jump drives—thumb-sized gizmos that hold thirty times the data that could be stored on my first computer—*all* of these labeled "Improv Book." I can't remember a time when I was not writing this book.

I want this fact to give you courage. As your improv guru shouldn't *I* be able to produce exciting results "on the spot," without an ounce of sweat, in real time? What on earth took me so long? Why didn't I just improvise this book? Actually, I did. Think about it. I've kept on saying *yes* to the voice that wanted to tell this story. I've *shown up* year after year, day after day to my writing desk. I've made whale-sized *mistakes* trying to find the right form for the message. (For years this was both a drama textbook and a self-help manual.) I've returned over and over to my purpose (*stay on course*) of writing a book that will share the mysteries of improvising with everyone, and I didn't stop until I found the perfect editor and publisher who understood and believed in the project. Plus, I have been *enjoying the ride,* thanks to all *the gifts* of support from my friends, students, and colleagues along the way. So you see, improvisations come in many sizes, forms, and time frames. Perhaps there is a great dream gathering dust on the shelf of your life. It is never too late to start it or make progress if it is under way but neglected.

I know that doing decades of improv play has confirmed me as a cockeyed optimist. I believe that people can change. I've seen it. Profound difficulties and bad habits are often surmountable. The phenomenal growth of the twelve-step programs worldwide is a testament to the determination of millions to improve how they live. If there is a change that you need to make I hope that the improv maxims have inspired you to get started.

When I gave up those paint-by-numbers kits years ago, I started on a different path. I'm grateful to the kit makers because their product got my hands moving with a paintbrush in the first place. In the half century since then, I've painted a lot of postcards. I know from experience that images appear, ideas pop into my head, and words come to me. What shows up on the paper is so often a wonderful surprise. Improv has trained me to be less concerned with outcomes and more interested in the process and in the quality of my relationships.

However, there *are* final products and endings to this work, and when I look at them I see not so much my handicraft as that of a greater source. My lesson has been that Polonius's advice, "To thine own self be true," isn't quite right. When I improvise it isn't *my* truth that comes to light, so much as the truth that includes all of those with whom I share this life, the truth of the moment. Working this way can connect us with the bigger picture, and we may be able to find a clearer sense of our role in the divine scheme of things. The privilege of life becomes more apparent.

I have always been moved by the Buddhist story of the blind turtle. It is a teaching fable designed to illustrate the concept of "precious human rebirth"—the wonder of the gift of human life. According to the legend, a man threw a wooden yoke into the sea, and it drifted around, tossed by winds east and west. Once every hundred years a blind turtle would rise from the bottom of the sea and swim to the surface. How often, do you imagine, will this turtle poke his head through the floating ring? These are the odds we have of being given a human rebirth, according to the ancients. It seems wrong to waste it, don't you think?

Years ago I wrote a fable to illustrate this urgency.

The Water Tank

In the small town of Tuvida, water allotment was legislated. When a child was born, the town council held a drawing and assigned the child's water allowance for life. The lottery was random, so one might receive anything from 100 to 100 million gallons. The water was stored in a giant cylinder in each person's backyard. There was a tap on the side of the tank. To the eye, everyone's tank appeared the same—it was enormous, and could easily hold enough water for seventy to a hundred years of use. The difference, of course, was that the amount of water *inside* each tank varied. And there was no way to determine how much that was.

The citizens of Tuvida dealt with this reality in a variety

of ways. One man kept records of all the water used by everyone for the past fifty years; he had created a chart showing the statistical probabilities for the amount of water each person was likely to have been given. Some townsfolk rationed the water parsimoniously, never even planting a garden for fear of overusing their supply; some put in hot tubs, water fountains, and swimming pools to celebrate their imagined bounty. One fellow built a huge lake for fishing, boating, and swimming to share with his neighborhood. However, the one thing that no one ever chose to do was to turn on the spigot and just let the water run freely. Of course, occasionally, while a person was watering his lawn he would forget, but no one consciously wasted it.

How would you use your water allotment if you lived in Tuvida? Think of the minutes in your life as drops of water from your tank. Your tap isn't dripping, is it?

What shall I do with this precious time, this improvisation that is my life? I'll bet you have some ideas. Improv points to ways of being more and better alive, ways of cutting through our patterns of procrastination and doubt. It is up to each of us, however, to make the move. No dream or goal is too large or too small. A life of meaning and value is achieved through purposeful action. Risk is involved. Feeling insecure is natural, expected—part of the territory. And while improvising won't guarantee perfect results, it does offer us the chance to join the party, to get on stage. And remember that there is lots of support out there.

Why waste another moment? Today is an ideal day to begin. I'm sure that you aren't waiting to come up with a perfect plan or to memorize all your lines before you start.

You know better now. Just jump on the stage of life and try/see. Then you will have earned your membership in our secret society of improvisers. I wish you good fortune and great adventures as you skip, jump, and stumble along this way. Step on stage. Take a bow. Have a good time.

Improvise!

acknowledgments

Improvisation is an oral tradition. Teachers create games and exercises and offer them to students and other teachers who in turn pass them on. The origin of a particular game is often unknown. I am part of this lively exchange, and I accept responsibility for any errors or omissions you may find. My purpose has been to share principles for living that derive from the playful study of improvising. The wisdom of improv is part of a stream of knowledge that stretches over time and crosses cultures.

To write this book I stood on the shoulders of two giants: Professor Keith Johnstone, maverick educator and theater innovator, and Dr. David K. Reynolds, anthropologist and Western authority on Japanese psychotherapies. Studying with these remarkable teachers has led to my understanding of improvisation and of life. Both have taught me to observe ordinary reality more carefully and to be kind. Both have modeled the power of action, the folly of self-absorption, and the habit of saying yes and thank you.

While the ideas in this book come through me, they are not mine. In particular, I use words, advice, and exercises gleaned from nearly two decades of association with Dr. Reynolds and his paradigm known as Constructive Living®. I have appropriated many of these concepts into the maxims for spontaneous living. I urge readers who find this perspective useful to seek out the works of Dr. Reynolds included in the bibliography. However, there is much in *Improv Wisdom* that is not pure CL theory or practice.

I have also commandeered ideas from the improvisation theories I learned while studying with Professor Johnstone. His groundbreaking book *Impro* changed my consciousness of both theater and education and set me on a new path. For more than twenty years I have been using his perspective on improvisation and teaching my students "the world according to Keith." The paradigms found in the work of these two men are now so much a part of my thinking that it is possible that I have shortchanged the credit due to them. If it seems so, I hope they will accept my apology.

I would like to acknowledge the master teachers who have etched their influence on me: Chungliang Al Huang, tai chi master and calligrapher; Professors Maylon Hepp and William Brasmer of Denison University; Mineru Sawada Sensei of the Oomoto Foundation, tea master and calligrapher; Rebecca Stockley, past dean of the Bay Area Theatresports™ School of Improv; and Gertrude Curtler, instructor of English, Virginia Commonwealth University.

I was lucky to have had encouraging parents, Harry Michael and Louise Ryan. My dad repeatedly told me I could do anything. Mama supported all my crazy adventures and travels. If I had ever said, "I'm going to the moon," she would have helped me pack and slipped a few dollars in my handbag. She was the first person I ever knew who always said yes.

Growing up in the urban South, my unorthodox hobby was collecting religions. Responding to a fervent request (I was twelve years old), my parents gave me permission to attend different churches. Going to the synagogue, the cathedral, the Baptist church, and the Quaker meeting house was my private anthropology. My habit was to pretend I was a member of the faith and sing, chant, or meditate along with the service, an early actress in the making. While I had little idea of the actual meaning of the prayers or forms, I was intrigued by the aesthetics. Clearly I was a doer rather than a scholar. Reading about Catholicism could never match the experience of the smell of the incense or the heady taste of the communion wine. I'm sure that I must have done things that were reserved for true believers, but I can't remember ever being corrected. I'm grateful to those clergy who didn't embarrass me by blowing my cover.

When it came time to pick a major at Westhampton College, I chose philosophy; it seemed the broadest canvas available and would offer the mountaintop view, I reasoned. Years later when I arrived in California, I saw that my mountain view, which had been pointed only toward Europe and Western cultural values, was now facing the mysterious East. My teachers and supporters were everywhere. My position at Stanford provided me with unique resources, and the San Francisco Bay Area became a treasure trove of Eastern thought and practice.

Marsh McCall and Jeff Wachtel, formerly of Stanford's Continuing Studies program, were the first at Stanford to sponsor my work teaching improvisation to adults. Charles Junkerman, the current dean of this program and associate provost of the university, has been an inspired and generous advocate for my work for over a decade. Without the thousands of Continuing Studies students I would never have been able to develop improv ideas in the classroom. The members of the Drama Department at Stanford, notably Professor Michael Ramsaur, allowed me to expand and explore the teaching of improvisation for undergraduates and provided resources for my group, the Stanford Improvisors. The recent senior lecturer–sabbatical leave policy, championed by the provost, Professor John Etchemendy, provided the needed time for my writing. I am grateful for this support and patronage.

Members of the San Francisco improvisation community have been my artistic mentors. I have studied with each of these talented professionals and owe much of my understanding of the art form to them: Cara Alter, Rafe Chase, Nan Crawford, Laura Derry, Dan Goldstein, William Hall, Carol Hazenfield, Stephen Kearin, Paul Killam, Kat Koppit, Brian Lohmann, Winter Mead, Diane Rachel, Regina Saisi, Barbara Scott, and Nina Wise. To the entire network of BATS, and the players of Pulp Playhouse, True Fiction Magazine, and 3 For All, I wish to express my appreciation. By showing up to perform week after week, you embody the wisdom that I have been trying to capture in this book. Thanks for many brave, astonishing moments of creation and laughter.

I have had financial support for my writing from unexpected sources. In particular, the gift of time made possible by a generous grant in 1995 from the late Billie Achilles of Palo Alto to my department provided me with leave time to devote to writing. I am grateful to David and Lynn Mitchell, who were instrumental in introducing us.

My Stanford students, especially the 160-plus members of the Stanford Improvisors, are due my very special thanks. Linda Roberts urged me to start the group in 1991 and have them play Theatresports™. Three of the founding members of the group deserve particular recognition. Ross McCall was responsible for the introduction that led to my work teaching adults. Dan Klein, a gifted teacher of improv, has been my backup over the years, and Adam Tobin showed up at exactly the right moment to brainstorm the planning for this book, giving generously of his time. My teaching assistants at Stanford have been there silently sweeping the path for me, lifting my status with their enthusiasm, and giving me Fridays off to write. Thanks to each of you.

Personal friendships have sustained and nourished me during the writing of this book—in particular I want to thank my women friends who have buoyed me along and cheered me on: Gail Boulanger, Trudy Boyle, Dalla Brown, Gail Grimes, Joan Madson, Lynn Reynolds, Sheila Saperstein, and Sylvia Usher.

Susan Mayse, a talented Canadian writer and editor, was an invaluable coach—she helped me to ask the question that uncovered the book I really needed to write. Finally, my imaginative and resourceful agent, Sarah Jane Freymann, brought me to the perfect editor, the amazing Toinette Lippe, who saw deeply into my purpose. Her playful wisdom, patience, attention to detail, and skill with language have inspired and instructed me. What incredible luck to have fallen under the tutelage of one of the most respected editors of spiritual books in America. I have been blessed to have had her guidance.

My final thanks are due my beloved husband, Ron, who is a gold medalist in goodness. He sat by my side at nearly a thousand performances, rubbed my feet when I got home late after teaching a ten-hour day, and always, always listened to my rambling. His kind, optimistic, capable, and encouraging presence in my life has helped me to be a sane enough person to write a book at all. He embodies all the best of improv wisdom in everything he does.

endnotes

1   Mick LaSalle, "Movies as Mirror," *San Francisco Chronicle*, May 9, 2004, 28.

2   David K. Reynolds, *Constructive Living* (Honolulu: University of Hawaii Press, 1984), 98.

3   The "Five Fears" list comes from an Indian Buddhist treatise, *Abhidarmakosha* by Vasubandhu. I am indebted to Professor Carl Bielefeldt of Stanford's Religious Studies Department for help in locating this citation.

4   Mary Rose O'Reilley, *Radical Presence* (Portsmouth, N.H.: Boynton/ Cook Publishers, 1998), 47.

5   Brenda Ueland, "Tell Me More: The Fine Art of Listening," *Utne Reader* 54, Nov./Dec. 1992, 104.

6   "Today's presents" is a variation on the first theme of Naikan: "What have I received from others?" For deeper study see the works of David K. Reynolds in the bibliography.

7   David K. Reynolds invented this game. I am indebted to him for teaching it to me.

8   The Preventive Medicine Research Institute, "Love and Survival," 2004, http://my.webmd.com/content/article/81/97068.ht.

9   Stephen Nachmanovitch, *Free Play: Improvisation in Art and Life* (Los Angeles: J. P. Tarcher), 1990, 94–95.

10 Bill McKibben, "Finding Meaning in an Age of Distraction: From the Personal to the Political," *Thirty Thousand Days: A Journal for Purposeful Living* 9, no. 3 (2003): 1.

11 Ibid.

12 David Dunn, *Try Giving Yourself Away* (Louisville, Ky: The Updegraff Press, 1998), 3.

13 Edward Espe Brown, *Tomato Blessings and Radish Teachings* (New York: Riverhead Books, 1997), 148.

14 Quotation found on Dr. Bradley Nieder's Web site: www.healthyhumorist.com/biography.htm

15 Rick Steves, *Rick Steves' Italy 2004* (Emeryville, Calif.: Avalon Travel, 2003), 37.

bibliography

Ackerman, Diane. *Deep Play*. New York: Random House, 1999.

Aoki, Hiroyuki. *Shintaido*. Shintaido of America, P.O. Box 22622, San Francisco, CA 94122, 1982.

Bergren, Mark, Molly Cox, and Jim Detmar. *Improvise This!: How to Think on Your Feet So You Don't Fall on Your Face*. New York: Hyperion, 2002.

Bernardi, Philip. *Improvisation Starters: A Collection of 900 Improvisation Situations for the Theater*. Cincinnati: Betterway Books, 1992.

Blofeld, John. *Bodhisattva of Compassion: The Mystical Tradition of Kuan Yin*. Boston: Shambhala, 1977.

———. *Taoism: The Road to Immortality*. Boulder, Colo.: Shambhala, 1978.

Boal, Augusto. *Games for Actors and Non-Actors*. London and New York: Routledge, 1992.

———. *The Rainbow of Desire*. London and New York: Routledge, 1995.

Chadwick, David. *Crooked Cucumber: The Life and Zen Teaching of Shunryu Suzuki*. New York: Broadway Books, 1999.

Coleman, Janet. *The Compass: The Improvisational Theatre That Revolutionized American Comedy*. Chicago: University of Chicago Press, 1990.

Dunn, David. *Try Giving Yourself Away*. Louisville, Ky.: The Updegraff Press, 1998.

Fischer, Norman. *Taking Our Places: The Buddhist Path to Truly Growing Up*. San Francisco: HarperSanFrancisco, 2003.

Foreman, Kathleen and Clem Martini. *Something Like a Drug: An Unauthorized Oral History of Theatresports*. Alberta, Canada: Red Deer College Press, 1995.

Fox, Jonathan. *Acts of Service: Spontaneity, Commitment, Tradition in the Nonscripted Theatre*. New Paltz, N.Y.: Tusitala Publishing, 1994.

Frost, Anthony and Ralph Yarrow. *Improvisation in Drama*. London: Macmillan, 1990.

Goldberg, Natalie. *Writing Down the Bones: Freeing the Writer Within*. Boston: Shambhala, 1986.

———. *Wild Mind: Living the Writer's Life*. New York: Bantam, 1990.

———. *Living Color: A Writer Paints Her World*. New York: Bantam, 1997.

Hall, William and Paul Killam, eds. *BATS Playbook*. BATS, B350 Fort Mason Center, San Francisco, CA 94123.

Halpern, Charna, Del Close, and Kim Johnson. *Truth in Comedy: The Manual of Improvisation*. Colorado Springs: Meriwether Publishing, 1993.

Hayward, Dr. Jeremy. "First Thought, Best Thought," *Tricycle Magazine*, Spring, 1995.

Hazenfield, Carol. *Acting on Impulse: The Art of Making Improv Theater*. Berkeley, Calif.: Coventry Creek Press, 2002.

Hodgson, John and Ernest Richards. *Improvisation*. New York: Grove Press, 1966.

Hyde, Lewis. *The Gift: Imagination and the Erotic Life of Property*. New York: Vintage Books, 1979.

Johnstone, Keith. *Impro: Improvisation and the Theatre*. New York: Theatre Arts Books, 1979.

———. *Impro for Storytellers*. New York: Routledge /Theatre Arts Books, 1999.

Kao, John J. *Jamming: The Art and Discipline of Business Creativity*. New York: HarperCollins, 1996.

Koppett, Kat. *Training to Imagine*. Sterling, Va.: Stylus, 2001.

Krech, Gregg. *Naikan: Gratitude, Grace, and the Japanese Art of Self-Reflection*. Berkeley, Calif.: Stone Bridge Press, 2002.

Lippe, Toinette. *Nothing Left Over: A Plain and Simple Life*. New York: J. P. Tarcher, 2002.

———. *Caught in the Act: Reflections on Being, Knowing, and Doing*. New York: J. P. Tarcher, 2004.

Lowe, Robert. *Improvisation, Inc.: Harnessing Spontaneity to Engage People and Groups*. San Francisco: Jossey-Bass/Pfeiffer, 2000.

Maguire, Jack. *The Power of Personal Storytelling: Spinning Tales to Connect with Others*. New York: J. P. Tarcher, 1998.

Maisel, Dr. Eric. *The Creativity Book*. New York: J. P. Tarcher, 2000.

Mathieu, W. A. *The Listening Book: Discovering Your Own Music*. Boston: Shambhala, 1991.

McKibben, Bill. *The Age of Missing Information*. New York: Random House, 1992.

Nachmanovitch, Stephen. *Free Play: Improvisation in Art and Life*. Los Angeles: J. P. Tarcher, 1990.

O'Reilley, Mary Rose. *Radical Presence*. Portsmouth, N.H.: Boynton/Cook, 1998.

Remen, Rachel Naomi. *My Grandfather's Blessings: Stories of Strength, Refuge, and Belonging*. New York: Riverhead Books, 2000.

Reynolds, Dr. David K. *The Quiet Therapies*. Honolulu: University of Hawaii Press, 1980.

———. *Naikan Psychotherapy: Meditation for Self-Development*. Chicago: University of Chicago Press, 1983.

———. *Constructive Living*. Honolulu: University of Hawaii Press, 1984.

———. *Playing Ball on Running Water*. New York: William Morrow, 1984.

———. *Even in Summer the Ice Doesn't Melt*. New York: William Morrow, 1986.

———. *Water Bears No Scars*. New York: William Morrow, 1987.

———. *Thirsty, Swimming in the Lake*. New York: William Morrow, 1991.

———. *Rainbow Rising from a Stream*. New York: William Morrow, 1992.

———. *A Handbook for Constructive Living*. Honolulu: University of Hawaii Press, 2001.

Salas, Jo. *Improvising Real Life: Personal Story in Playback Theatre*. Dubuque, Iowa: Kendall/Hunt, 1993.

Spolin, Viola. *Improvisation for the Theatre*. Evanston, Ill.: Northwestern University Press, 1963.

———. *Theatre Games for Rehearsal*. Evanston, Ill.: Northwestern University Press, 1985.

Stockley, Rebecca and Lynda Belts. *Improvisation Through Theatresports*. Puyallup, Wash.: Thespis Productions, 1991.

Sweet, Jeffrey. *Something Wonderful Right Away*. Pompton Plains, N.J.: Limelight, 1986.

Tarrant, John. *Bring Me the Rhinocerous*. New York: Harmony Books, 2004.

Tharp, Twyla. *The Creative Habit: Learn It and Use It for Life*. New York: Simon & Schuster, 2003.

Weiner, Dr. Daniel. *Rehearsals for Growth: Theater Improvisation for Psychotherapists*. New York: W. W. Norton, 1994.

Wirth, Jeff. *Interactive Acting: Acting, Improvisation, and Interacting for Audience Participatory Theatre*. Fall Creek, Ore.: Fall Creek Press, 1994.

Wise, Nina. *A Big New Free Happy Unusual Life*. New York: Broadway Books, 2002.

Zaporah, Ruth. *Action Theater*. Berkeley, Calif.: North Atlantic Books, 1995.

Zarrilli, Phillip. *Acting (Re)Considered*. London and New York: Routledge, 1995.

resources

BAY AREA THEATRESPORTS™
B350 Fort Mason Center
San Francisco, CA 94123
Phone: (415) 474-8935
E-mail: info@improv.org; Web site: www.improv.org

CONSTRUCTIVE LIVING RESOURCES
Dr. David K. Reynolds Web site:
http://boat.zero.ad.jp/~zbe85163/
California Center for Constructive Living Web site:
www.constructiveliving.com
Canadian Center for Constructive Living Web site:
www.constructiveliving.ca

STANFORD UNIVERSITY CONTINUING STUDIES PROGRAM
Stanford, CA 94305
Phone: (650) 725-2650
Web site: http://continuingstudies.stanford.edu/

THE INTERNATIONAL THEATRESPORTS™ INSTITUTE
P.O. Box 82084
Calgary, AB T3C 3W5, Canada
Phone: (403) 246-5496
E-mail: admin@theatresports.org
Web site: www.theatresports.org

IMPROV WEBRING
Web site: www.mindspring. com/~bsack/webring.html

RESOURCES FOR BUSINESS APPLICATIONS
Web site: http://appliedimprov.com

CONTACT THE AUTHOR
E-mail: improvwisdom@gmail.com
Web sites: www.stanford.edu/~patryan; www.improvwisdom.com

finding an improvisation class

Since improvising is a social art, the best way to study it is by working in a group. Taking a class in improvising is ideal, if you can locate one in your area. If you live in a metropolitan area in the United States or Europe, chances are that there is an improvisation class (or many) being taught near you. Check local entertainment listings to find the names of improvisational theater groups in your area first. Often these groups offer classes to the public or will know where improvisation is being taught. A phone call to their box office may put you in contact with a teacher.

Continuing Studies programs, adult learning centers, and university extension divisions are likely to host classes and workshops. Theater training programs and university drama departments typically have resources for improv or can guide you to them.

The Internet is a vast resource of improv information. The Improv Webring (see Resources) is a clearinghouse for URLs relating to improvisation. It is a good starting place. If research doesn't turn up a local class, consider starting your own group. You might seek out someone with improv knowledge or experience to help you; any educational program with a drama department, including a high school, might have faculty who could help.

Keith Johnstone's wonderful book *Impro for Storytellers* is the best book I know as a guide for improv games and exercises. The classic *Improvisation for the Theatre* by Viola Spolin contains hundreds of such games. And, of course, it's great to improvise and make up your own games and challenges. The important thing is to enjoy the process. Remember that there are no wrong answers.

about the author

Patricia Ryan Madson has been teaching for nearly half a century. On the Stanford Drama faculty since 1977, she founded the Stanford Improvisors in 1991. As head of the undergraduate acting program, she won the university's highest teaching prize, the Lloyd W. Dinkelspiel Award for outstanding contribution to undergraduate education. She teaches regularly at the Esalen Institute, at the California Institute for Transpersonal Psychology, and for Stanford's Continuing Studies program. For a decade she was the American coordinator for the Oomoto School of Traditional Japanese Arts in Kameoka, Japan.

Patricia lives with her husband, Ronald Madson, and their Himalayan cat, Buddha, in El Granada, California, where they direct the California Center for Constructive Living. *Improv Wisdom* is her first book.